T0248225

YOU
BETTER
WATCH
OUT

ALSO BY JAMES S. MURRAY AND DARREN WEARMOUTH

Awakened
The Brink
Obliteration
Don't Move
The Stowaway

YOU BETTER WATCH OUT

JAMES S. MURRAY
AND DARREN WEARMOUTH

ST. MARTIN'S PRESS
NEW YORK

First published in the United States by St. Martin's Press, an imprint of St. Martin's Publishing Group

YOU BETTER WATCH OUT. Copyright © 2024 by James S. Murray and Darren Wearmouth. All rights reserved. Printed in the United States of America. For information, address St. Martin's Publishing Group, 120 Broadway, New York, NY 10271.

www.stmartins.com

Library of Congress Cataloging-in-Publication Data

Names: Murray, James S. (James Stephen), 1976– author. | Wearmouth, Darren, author.
Title: You better watch out / James S. Murray and Darren Wearmouth.
Description: First edition. | New York : St. Martin's Press, 2024.
Identifiers: LCCN 2024019624 | ISBN 9781250286260 (hardcover) | ISBN 9781250286277 (ebook)
Subjects: LCGFT: Thrillers (Fiction) | Novels.
Classification: LCC PS3613.U763 Y68 2024 | DDC 813/.6—dc23/eng/20240426
LC record available at https://lccn.loc.gov/2024019624

Our books may be purchased in bulk for promotional, educational, or business use. Please contact your local bookseller or the Macmillan Corporate and Premium Sales Department at 1-800-221-7945, extension 5442, or by email at MacmillanSpecialMarkets@macmillan.com.

First Edition: 2024

10 9 8 7 6 5 4 3

For Jim & Maryann Murray

YOU
BETTER
WATCH
OUT

1

Darkness had invaded Old Forge.

Snowflakes sprinkled Eddie Parker's windshield as he drove along Main Street. The small Upstate New York town had a homely feel. Retro streetlights giving off warm yellow glows. Adorable local stores stuffed with holiday decorations. He imagined that most of the inhabitants were straight out of a Norman Rockwell painting, gathered around their fires on this cold Christmas-week evening. Most places had closed for the night and the sidewalks were deserted.

Old Forge had heaps of character, and its quaintness drew people from miles around. It was a tourist trap in the summer, with the best boat tours in the Adirondacks. But it had the lowest temperatures in the entire state during the winter. Truly brutal weather. Even so, Eddie never tired of seeing the place on his drive back from his brother's cabin.

Also, the people here had money. Lots of it. Eddie had a maxed-out credit card, forty bucks in his wallet, and was a month behind on his rent. But he knew he had a few more months to go before his landlord could start the eviction process. New York law was a bitch to landlords, thankfully. But overall, a pretty sad situation for a thirty-year-old guy. Once back home, he vowed to get a *real* job.

Because Lord knows, he had done his old job for *far* too long. It was time for a change.

A bright sign beamed at the end of the strip. The local grocery store had remained open.

And he needed a pack of smokes.

On a cold winter night, it was a match made in heaven.

Eddie slowed and flicked on his turn signal.

The store entrance swung open, sending a shaft of light into the street. A man walked out with a couple of six-packs.

He pulled into the dilapidated parking lot at the side of the building. Moments after, a set of headlights flashed past his SUV. A minivan parked a few spots to his left. It had a blue wheelchair sign in one of its windows.

Eddie sensed an opportunity. Maybe the "real" job search could start tomorrow . . .

A silver-haired lady, dressed in a thick coat, struggled out of the driver's side. She unsteadily made her way around to the other side of the minivan. A minute later, she reappeared with a stick-thin husband in an electric wheelchair. The couple was maybe in their seventies. Probably too old to brave this kind of weather for butterscotch candies and a bottle of Bartles & Jaymes.

Eddie scanned the place for any security cameras.

Nothing.

For a moment, he kicked himself for allowing another one of his bad habits to surface, but quickly rationalized the moment.

One last score to see me through Christmas.

Besides, nobody'll get hurt.

Nobody will ever get hurt again.

He jumped out of his vehicle, and his breath instantly fogged in the frigid night air. His jeans and a sweater provided poor protection from the elements.

Eddie broke into a jog toward the entrance, following the wheelchair tracks in the snow. He dragged open the door and stepped into the welcoming warmth.

Quiet Christmas music leaked out from an old, dilapidated speaker. It looked like a Radio Shack special, circa Black Friday 1994. The woman at the checkout glanced at him, then focused back on a wall-mounted tube TV playing repeats of *Wheel of Fortune*.

The tiny grocery store had a measly five aisles. The elderly couple moved along the one farthest from the counter. The old woman's basket was already half-full and she visibly struggled with its weight. Eddie followed closely behind, glancing back and forth between his targets and the various junk foods on display. The freshest seemed to be the Twinkies. The hot dogs on the roller looked like they needed carbon dating.

The couple moved along to the next aisle. They seemed in good spirits, busily chatting while completely unaware of his presence. The perfect marks.

The bell at the front door of the store tinkled.

He paused his pursuit by the refrigerators.

A middle-aged cop with a stern stare had walked in. The type of humorless asshole that would give you a ticket for looking at him the wrong way. It was the last thing Eddie needed on a night like this, but he told himself to play it cool.

"Sheriff Briggs," the old man called out.

"George. Dorothy. What you doing out on a night like this?"

"You know how Dorothy likes to stock up for the holiday, Sheriff," the old man said with a smile.

"The roast isn't going to cook itself," the woman replied, pinching her husband's side lovingly.

"Do you have a moment, Sheriff?" the old man asked.

"I'm in a bit of a rush, sadly."

"Nothing too serious, we hope?"

"Oh no, just a minor incident on the other side of town. What's up?"

"We were watching the news last night and wanted to congratulate you on another year of no murders in Old Forge."

The cop gave her a satisfying nod. "Oh, don't thank me, George, Dorothy. It's the good people that live here that make all the difference, such as the two of you."

Eddie half-listened to the conversation, biding his time nearby.

He pretended to check out the cans of generic vegetables and dusty boxes of Froot Loops. The cop hustled over to the checkout, bought a lottery ticket—so not in that much of a rush—and strode back outside, seemingly without a care in the world. Moments later, his cruiser casually pulled away from the front of the store.

The old couple continued through the aisles, picking a few more items. The basket looked ready to burst, though it contained nothing of interest. Finally, they headed over to the register.

Eddie moved directly behind them. He hated himself for doing this.

He had learned the dark arts of theft as a teenager. It required patience. No matter how vigilant or attentive someone might be, the perfect opportunity to rob them always came along.

He edged forward to closely watch their every move. Their every detail. But not close enough to arouse suspicion. The old lady wrestled the basket onto the counter. Her husband was wearing a pricey-looking suit under his overcoat. Eddie doubted his plan would put a serious dent in their finances.

More likely, they'd simply get over it.

The server scanned the items and put them in several plastic bags.

Patience.

Do this outside.

The old lady opened her Chanel purse.

Excitement shot through Eddie's body.

It was crammed with cash.

At least a few grand, he figured. Enough to survive until he found work.

She pulled out a hundred-dollar bill and paid for the items. But as the old woman struggled to lift the grocery bags, one slipped from her frail hand, sending cans rattling across the tiled floor.

Eddie immediately bent down to pick them up. His playing the Good Samaritan meant they wouldn't see what was coming next.

"Thank you, young man," she said. "I hate to ask, but would you be a dear and help us to the car? These groceries seem to get heavier and heavier each year."

"Of course, my pleasure," Eddie replied.

"You're a gentleman," the old man said. "Not enough of those going around much anymore."

Eddie smiled at the couple warmly.

The perfect opportunity.

This was gonna be smooth sailing. He swept the remaining bags off the counter and followed the couple outside.

The man's electric wheelchair left two fresh trails in the

snow-covered ground. The woman waddled beside him as they headed into the dark parking lot.

"Where are you from, young man?" she asked.

"Fort Drum, born and bred, ma'am."

"Really? What brings you to our little town?"

"Oh, just cruising through. Eager to get home for the holiday, see the family, know what I mean?"

The elderly lady smiled. "Well, don't worry, my husband and I won't keep you for long. But we're so glad you came through Old Forge."

They stopped by the side of the minivan. The old woman slid open the side door, placed her purse on the seat, and folded out a ramp. She hit a button on the key fob, opening the trunk.

"You know," the old man said, "we always need more people like you."

"People like me?"

He nodded and smiled. "Yes, son. Just like you."

"Be a good man and place the groceries in the back," his wife added.

Eddie glanced around to make sure the coast was clear.

Nobody had followed them into the quiet parking lot. The few cars around them had a foot of snow on top. No headlights brightened the visible stretch of road outside the store.

This was his moment. He was easily too fast for them, and his prize lay within an arm's reach. The easiest score of his life. This time, with zero collateral damage.

He dumped the shopping bags he was holding. Rushed around to the front of the wheelchair. Thrust his arm inside the vehicle to grab the purse. In a moment, he would be gone, and flush with cash.

Instead, he felt a sharp scratch on the side of his neck.

Eddie planted his hand against the sudden pain.

He spun to face the old couple, confused over what had just happened.

The old man had risen from his wheelchair, now looking tall and composed. He took a step back from Eddie, holding a syringe in his right hand. The woman had also retreated a few paces. The friendly smiles had now disappeared from their faces, replaced with expressions of grim curiosity.

"What the fuck," he muttered.

Eddie lurched toward the couple, but his right leg buckled. He collapsed to one knee, gasping for breath but unable to stand.

Energy drained from his body.

His eyelids wilted.

Desperate, he threw out a flailing arm that brushed against the old man's polished shoes.

Eddie tried with every remaining ounce of energy to move. To get the hell away from whatever was happening. Instead, with all power sapped from him and his vision blurring, he dropped face-first into the snow.

Then . . . his world went black.

2

E ddie's head felt like it was about to explode. His body shivered on the freezing ground. Every muscle ached. He swallowed hard to moisten his parched throat. A biting wind whipped against the back of his wet clothes, sending a shudder down his spine. His hands tightened into fists as he attempted to collect his thoughts.

Images swirled in his mind, eventually crystallizing into coherent thoughts. Driving home at night. Old Forge. The grocery store. A purse packed with cash.

George and Dorothy.

They'd taken him out in a matter of seconds.

The old couple hadn't been simply defending themselves. A spray of Mace in his eyes? He could get that. But who carried syringes in their pockets, primed with a powerful drug, ready to inject into a thief . . .

His eyes slammed open, mind racing over the last thing he remembered. It took a few seconds for his vision to clear. A few more seconds to register his surroundings. This wasn't the parking lot or Old Forge. It looked even more historic.

Ornate streetlights lined the sidewalks at irregular intervals. Snow drove through their dazzling yellow ambience and blasted against his shivering body.

Eddie groaned to a crouch on a cobblestone street. He let out a rasping breath. Wrapped his arms around himself for warmth, glancing in both directions. One end of the road disappeared into utter darkness. For a moment he wondered if the old couple had left him in a deserted hamlet, miles from anywhere, to teach him a lesson. The other end of the road led to a brightly lit town square.

But . . .

There were no cars . . . No people in sight . . . No signs of life anywhere.

What the hell?

Weak lights bled out of several buildings. Every one of them had hokey Christmas decorations in their windows, reminiscent of a bygone era. A few of the storefronts looked vaguely familiar, like the pharmacy and the diner, but he couldn't place them in time or space. It was more like a memory from childhood, invoked by a song or a phrase.

Eddie winced at the pain from the cold. He needed to get inside—anywhere—to establish where he was and find a way home.

He pawed at his jean pockets. Empty.

The old couple must have taken his cell phone and wallet.

What the hell . . .

An old-time saloon lay directly to his right, resembling something he imagined from the early part of the twentieth century. Thin light radiated out of its four windows. A set of wooden steps led underneath a veranda toward the entrance. It looked like the type of place where the customers wouldn't appreciate a stranger's presence. Then again, Eddie wasn't welcome in *most* places, whether he was a stranger or not.

His limited options meant braving the cold and likely catching hypothermia, or braving the locals and getting run out of town.

He opted for the locals. Most Upstaters didn't have pitchforks.

A strong gust of wind roared through the street, shrouding him in a cloud of snow. He climbed to his feet, still woozy from whatever drug he had been injected with. He was guessing it was propofol, or something similar.

He stumbled to the sidewalk in front of the bar, like a drunk looking for a late night spot to keep the party going. He clambered up the saloon steps and shoved the doors open forcefully.

Eddie had expected raucous locals drinking it up after a long day's work in the terrible storm outside. The clack of pool balls. Terrible music thumping out of a jukebox. Maybe a few heads whipping in his direction as he entered, checking out the stranger in town.

Instead, the bar was completely empty.

The odors of timber and burning oil instantly hit him. His boots creaked over the wooden floorboards as he advanced into the room.

A distant choral version of "Silent Night" came from somewhere in the bar. The volume was low but distinguishable. The track had the distinctive, soothing crackle of an old-time record player.

The soft tones were out of place in a small-town bar.

He slowly turned in a complete circle. All of the tables inside were empty, though several had beer glasses on them. The long-paneled bar at the side of the room had tinsel taped all around it, but no barkeep stood behind the faded taps.

Eddie cupped his hands around his mouth and breathed on them for warmth. He scanned the apparently abandoned establishment for any hint of life.

The lighting in the saloon came from three lit kerosene lamps. One had been placed on the corner of the bar. Another sat on a table by the window. The third was on top of a dark jukebox.

The bar had electricity, though, meaning the place wasn't dead to the world. A string of multicolored Christmas lights had been hung around a pitiful-looking plastic Christmas tree.

"Hello?" Eddie called out, baffled by the entire experience.

Nobody replied.

If the *Mary Celeste* had been on dry land, this would be it.

The record spun to a finish, leaving only the sound of the endless crackle.

Wait a second . . .

Someone must have been here. Recently. The kerosene lamps and the record player told him that much.

None of this made sense.

For a moment, he wondered if he was dreaming.

Dream or not, his priorities were clear.

Get warm and dry.

Call my brother for a ride back to Fort Drum.

Get the fuck outta here.

Eddie weaved between the empty tables and approached the bar. A seven-inch single spun on the record player. He frowned. From memory, he knew this could've only lasted a few minutes at most. So who had played the track?

A door lay to his right, probably leading to a kitchen or a stockroom in the back.

"Yo," he shouted. "Anyone home?"

Once again, nobody replied.

He racked his brain for answers.

None of this feels real.

Where the hell did the old couple leave me?

A sense of danger rose inside him.

Eddie stooped below the counter and entered the bar. The two fridges were powerless and empty. Dusty glasses filled the shelves. Old tin signs for Guinness, Budweiser, and Harley-Davidson hung on the wall. On closer inspection, they were reproductions. A brown dial phone sat next to a cash register that was fit for the Wild West.

His instinct drew him to a knife on a chopping board. It was the best thing he could see for self-defense. He grabbed it with his still-shivering hand, peering around the empty room for any signs of movement. Any hint of reality in this warped place.

Suddenly, a scream split the air. Piercing and loud. The type he recognized as someone scared out of their mind.

Eddie hunched down to hide behind the bar. The scream had come from behind the backroom door. He considered his options for a second. First, running out into the freezing night with no idea where he was going. But that could leave him miles from anywhere.

Second, discovering the source and reason for the scream.

The voice had sounded like a woman—one who was in imminent danger.

The devil on his shoulder told him to flee. Save his own skin. Get out of Dodge before seeking out any more trouble.

Eddie shook his head. "Goddammit."

It sounded like she needed help.

And if he was being honest, he needed help too.

He ducked out from behind the bar and quietly strode toward the door, knife clutched firmly in his hand. He took a deep breath, mentally preparing himself for war.

With a powerful thrust of his leg, he kicked open the back door, ready for anything.

3

Eddie's heart pounded against his chest as the door burst open. In front of him, another kerosene lamp had been placed on top of a freezer, dimly lighting the room. He cautiously entered, knife ready to slash at anyone who attacked.

A woman, a few years younger than him, lay sprawled on the kitchen's vinyl floor. She was knocked out cold, and was wearing a pair of hiking pants and a hoodie. Definitely not the correct clothing for the harsh weather outside. Blood had soaked her brown ponytail and pooled around her head.

She seemed to be in the same predicament as him, but with worse injuries than a severely dented ego and a headache.

Eddie took a tentative step toward her, adrenaline surging through him.

A sharp intake of breath broke the silence in the kitchen.

He spun to face another small-framed woman. Her chest heaved, making the thick gold chain around her neck glint. Sweat beaded on her dark skin. She sat staring at him for a heartbeat, then scrambled away on her backside until she crashed against a stove. From here, it looked like she was wearing a pair of fleece pajamas. Also sorely underdressed for the occasion.

"Stay away from me!" she yelled at Eddie.

What the hell is going on here?

It appeared that she hadn't struck the other woman.

Eddie quickly searched the room for the attacker, but there was no one else there. He focused back on the conscious woman. Tucked his knife into a neutral position and took a step forward, hands raised.

She reached up and grabbed an empty beer bottle from a cooking station. "You move any closer, I'll shove this right up your ass."

"Whoa, whoa, whoa," Eddie replied. "I'm not here to hurt you."

"Could've fooled me, asshole."

"Listen, lady, I don't even know you!" Eddie implored. "I woke up out on the freezing cold street, like five minutes ago. I came into that weird-ass bar out there, and then heard you scream. That's it."

"You're full of shit."

"Just look at me! My story clearly checks out."

She carefully eyed his soaking-wet clothes and shivering body. "What happened to you?"

"The fuck if I know, lady."

"Did you get kidnapped too?"

"Kidnapped?" Eddie asked rhetorically, thinking back to his last memories in the parking lot. "I guess so, yeah. Did you just wake up?"

"Uh-huh. I screamed when I saw her body on the floor. Where the fuck are we?"

"I don't know. It's like some bar in this small town . . . but not like a modern bar. The place looks ancient. And . . ."

The woman waited in anticipation for Eddie's next words.

"The whole place is deserted. I mean, it seems like the whole *town*. I don't get it."

"What? Did you see a gas station outside? Anything like that?"

"Everywhere looked closed apart from here. No cars. No pedestrians. No clue where the hell we are."

"What's your last memory?" the woman asked.

"That's the least of our worries at the moment."

The last thing he wanted to do was tell her the truth, that he was about to mug a couple of old folks after helping carry their Christmas shopping. The tiny grain of trust between them would certainly disappear once the truth came out.

She nervously gazed around the kitchen, taking rapid breaths. Eddie moved back to the doorway and checked to see if anyone had entered the saloon. He didn't believe in coincidences. Everything had a reason. But this? The bizarreness of it all terrified him.

"Do you have a phone?" he asked.

She gave a forlorn shake of the head. "That's the first thing I checked."

He walked back toward her. Extended a hand and hauled her up. "Eddie Parker. I'd say great to meet you but . . ."

"Trinity Jackson."

"How did you get here?"

She shrugged unknowingly.

"Are you injured?"

"I don't think so."

"Okay. Then let's see what her story is," Eddie said, motioning to the unconscious girl on the floor.

He grabbed the kerosene lamp from the freezer and rushed back to her side. He crouched down and visually inspected her for wounds. Her body appeared fine, but she'd taken a sharp blow to the side of the head.

"Do you have medical training?" Eddie asked Trinity.

"No. Do you?"

"Hardly."

Eddie grabbed the injured woman's wrist and found a pulse.

He hovered his hand over her nose and mouth. She was still breathing and had a heartbeat. That was all he could tell.

He headed back into the bar area and swept a glass off a table. Returned to the kitchen, placed it underneath a rusty faucet, and twisted. A piercing metallic screech reverberated around the room, but no water came out.

"Ouch," Trinity said, recoiling at the unpleasant noise. "Sink busted?"

"I suppose. If it ever worked to begin with."

Eddie scoured the various drawers and closets in the kitchen, searching for a first aid kit. All he discovered was a broom and a beer towel. He knelt back by the injured woman and cupped her head in his hand. Scrunched the towel and gently dabbed it against the swollen part. She had one hell of a nasty bruise.

After a few seconds, she winced.

Then her eyes flickered open.

Jess's head pounded. A high-pitched sound filled her ears. Everything looked like it was underwater. The figure of a man knelt by her side with a bloodstained towel in his hand. Behind him, a woman frantically glanced between her and the open door.

She blinked a few times to clear her vision.

The man edged away.

Jess raised a quivering hand toward the side of her head. The agonizing pain made her grimace. It felt like somebody had dropped an anvil on her skull.

"Hey, can you hear me?" the man asked, his voice coming into focus in her mind. "Are you okay?"

She attempted to get up, but her body slumped back against the floor.

"Whoa, take it easy," the strange man said.

"How did I . . . Who are you?" she muttered.

"My name is Eddie, and this is Trinity."

The woman kept watching Jess from the other side of the room. She tried to shake the fog out of her mind.

"I don't . . . What happened?" she asked. "Where am I? How did I get here?"

"I've got no idea—we're in the same boat as you. Minus the concussion."

Jess summoned all of her strength and groaned to a sitting position. The world around her cleared, including the pool of blood by her right hand.

"I promise you, it wasn't me," the man said. "Both of us just woke up here, just like you."

"He's lying," Trinity called from behind. "He said he came in from the street."

He shot her a glare. "You know what I meant. This place." Eddie waved his arms all around. "Yes, I woke up in the snow on the street outside."

"Where are we?" Jess asked.

"Don't know. But we're in the back of a deserted bar in what looks like a deserted town in the middle of a goddamn blizzard. We haven't seen a single other person—"

"He told me he hasn't seen anyone else," Trinity interrupted. "I've been in here the entire time, so we don't know if that's true or not."

"Would you shut up for a minute?" Eddie said, his frustration with Trinity growing by the minute.

He locked eyes with Jess. "Look. As I said, I'm Eddie. She's Trinity. I just met her. She thinks she was kidnapped. I clearly was too. Last thing I remember was being attacked in Old Forge."

Jess peered into the saloon. It seemed no one else was here. Eddie and Trinity both appeared to be in a blind panic, unaware of their location and unfamiliar with the strange surroundings. She could tell they'd be of no help. She would have to figure this out on her own. Neither one of them could be trusted, yet.

"My name is Jessica Kane." She grabbed a drawer handle and dragged herself to her feet. For a moment, she felt dizzy, and thrust an arm against a hot plate to maintain her balance. "The last thing I remember was hiking in the forest. I think somebody hit me from behind. What about you guys?"

"I was catching some z's," Trinity said. "Next thing, some guy breaks into my bedroom, jumps on top of me, and forces a damp cloth over my nose and mouth."

"Chloroform?" Eddie asked.

"Dunno. I fought like crazy for a few moments before I blacked out."

"Was it an old guy? Thin and in his seventies?"

"No. I mean, no way. This guy was strong. Why do you ask?"

"That's who injected me."

Jess took a groaning step toward Eddie. "Injected you? What happened?"

"I helped an elderly couple with their groceries in town. The old guy pretended to be in an electric wheelchair."

"Pretended?"

"Yeah. When I went to put the bags in the trunk, he stood up and shoved a needle in my neck. I think they lured me in."

"What do you mean?" Trinity pressed.

He paused for a moment, eyeing each of them. It gave Jess

YOU BETTER WATCH OUT **19**

the impression that he was holding something back, though it didn't matter right now.

"They purposefully asked for my help in the store," he eventually said. "If I didn't know any better, I'd say I was being cased. And if your story is true, Trinity—"

"Why the hell would I lie about it?" she snapped.

"The point I'm making is this. You were apparently taken by a different person than me, but all three of us were left in the same place. We don't know by whom, but there's more than one kidnapper. So, our top priority is to get the fuck out of this town before whoever they are return. Agreed?"

"I'm down with that," Trinity said.

"Don't suppose you've seen a daypack lying around?" Jess asked. "It had my phone and keys in it."

"Doubt you'll find it," Eddie replied. "Both of ours were taken."

Jess glanced around the dark kitchen. "Then let's grab weapons. And anything we can use. Clothes. Water. See if there's any way to call the cops before we head out."

The three of them nodded in agreement and scoured the room.

Jess took a few aching steps toward an industrial freezer, groaning as she opened its door. Eddie and Trinity checked out other parts of the kitchen, finding dusty plates and posters from a bygone age.

"Looks like this place hasn't been used in years," he said.

Jess shook her head. "Is it the same in the saloon?"

"Dunno. I think so. I mean, I barely had time to check things out."

"Well then, let's see what we've got."

She reached for the door.

Eddie threw an arm across her chest. "Wait."

"What?"

"There's something both of you should know. When I first entered the bar, there was a record player playing a song."

"So?" Trinity said.

"It means that someone else was in here."

She scowled at him. "No shit, Sherlock. How do you think we ended up in an abandoned bar?"

"No, I mean *very recently*. It was playing a single track."

Jess looked at the other two, worried. "So . . . we're not alone."

4

The three of them stared through the doorway into the abandoned bar. Their breaths clouded in the air.

Eddie squeezed the knife's handle with his shaking hand. A mix of cold and fear consumed him. He'd never felt so physically and mentally exposed in his life. The realization hit home that the person who had left him on the road could've been yards away, watching from a dark alley. The blizzard probably concealed any footprints in the snow.

Is this some sort of test?

"We can't stay in the kitchen," Jess whispered. "We have to check this place out."

"Why?" Trinity shot back. "What if we're walking into a trap? Playing right into their hands? You wanna be a detective, you go, girl. I'm staying right here."

"I'm not waiting for whatever they have planned," Eddie said. "We were left here for a reason."

"What reason?" Trinity asked. "None of this makes any fucking sense."

"I don't disagree with you. But we need to figure it out, and fast."

Trinity's constant questioning was annoying Eddie more and more. They were all flying blind, and the solution wasn't negativity. He walked into the saloon. The building's structure creaked in the wind. He gazed up at the thick wooden beams that ran across the ceiling. Outside, the blizzard continued to howl past the windows.

The group had to move.

The problem was, outside looked perilous and inside the saloon, danger filled the air.

Eddie thought about what he had encountered since waking.

"The phone!" he blurted.

Jess's head snapped in his direction. "Where?"

"Behind the bar. I saw a phone."

It seemed like a long shot based on what they'd already seen, but it was better than no shot. He raced across the groaning floorboards, ducked underneath the service hatch, and headed past the empty fridges.

Jess and Trinity crept over to the front of the bar. Both kept glancing toward the main entrance with understandable fear in their eyes. But if anyone burst into the bar to attack, Eddie liked his chances with the knife.

Unless they brought a gun . . .

He picked up the rotary phone's handset and planted it to his ear.

No dial tone.

He pressed the switch hooks a couple of times.

Still nothing.

The phone's cord ran underneath the bar. He gave it a gentle tug and it loosely swung into the bar area.

"What the hell?" he murmured.

Eddie ducked down to check if there was a connection. He found only a bottle opener and a screwdriver. He slid the tools over to Jess.

"Well?" Trinity asked.

"The goddamn thing is fake."

"Whaddaya mean?"

"Put here as a decoration. It's a dummy phone. Look." He flipped the device over, and it was simply a hollow shell. No inner workings or mechanisms at all. "It's like a prop phone you'd see in a movie."

Eddie stepped over to the cash register, scanning everything closely. "Look around you. There's no liquor in the bottles. There's dust on the tables. This place hasn't been used in years."

"I don't think it's *ever* been used," Jess added, peering around the weird room. "But they bothered to put up a Christmas tree?"

Eddie opened the register's drawer, revealing the empty compartments. The vintage keys also had a thin covering of dust.

He turned toward the back of the bar. A tattered old dollar bill had been tacked to the wall. On closer inspection, it was a relatively new 2019 series bill, maybe mangled and stained to purposely look dated.

"Guys," he said. "Come check this out."

Jess and Trinity stooped underneath the hatch and joined him.

Eddie pointed at the bill. "The date says 2019, but somebody weathered the money to look decades old. It's as fake as the phone."

Trinity's eyes narrowed. "Why would anyone do that?"

"No idea. But it's creeping me out," Jess said.

"You weren't creeped out already?"

"You know what I mean."

Eddie opened a few of the small cupboards. Again, nothing. Jess's theory about the bar's never having been open to the public was more plausible than its being closed for years.

But why?

What is this place?

Jess pointed to the opposite side of the room. "Guys, take a look at those."

To the left of the Christmas tree, two black-and-white photographs had been framed and hung on the wall. Each had writing beneath. From here, though, it was too hard to make out any details in the murky light.

The group headed over to check them out.

The first was a map of Old Forge, New York, circa 1937. Back then, the place had only a few roads. The contours had been drawn on the surrounding hills.

"I can tell you right now," Eddie said. "We're not in Old Forge."

"Did anything seem familiar outside?"

"Vaguely. I mean, it was hard to see past fifty feet with the blizzard."

The next photograph had "Main Street—Winter, 1936" written at the bottom.

Eddie leaned closer. It appeared similar to what he had seen outside. He headed straight over to a front window and surveyed the road.

"Jesus Christ," he breathed.

No, the photograph didn't just look close in appearance.

It was almost an exact match, down to the pharmacy and the diner. The town looked like a re-creation of Old Forge from nearly a century ago.

For the next few moments, he searched for any signs of movement. Any footprints in the snow. Something to give him a clue to their whereabouts. In the end, only one course of action kept jumping to the front his mind.

In a dark corner of the room, he spotted a standing rack with a few coats dangling off the hooks. Eddie grabbed the three thickest ones. They stunk like damp clothes that been left in the washing machine for a few days, but they would have to do.

He wrestled on the dark gray bomber. Headed back over to Trinity and Jess and held out the other two coats. "It's time to go," he said anxiously.

"What did you find?" Jess asked.

Eddie paused. "We're in Old Forge, all right."

"Huh?" Trinity said. "I know that place. But it looks nothing like outside."

"You're right. Not anymore."

"What do you mean?" Jess asked.

Eddie shook his head, not believing what he was about to actually say. "We're in Old Forge, circa 1936."

Trinity glared at him. "What kind of *Back to the Future* bullshit is this?"

"I'm not suggesting time travel—the dollar bill tells us that much. The town is a replica from the past. Someone built all this."

The three of them stared at each other, trying to process their bizarre reality.

"Well, this is just freaking fantastic," Trinity said. "I say we flag down a car. Find a phone. Knock on a door. Knock on all the damn doors. Something."

"Agreed," Jess replied.

The three of them headed to the front of the bar.

For a brief moment, everyone gazed out of the window at the snow-swept cobblestone street. Eddie knew danger probably lurked outside, but he had a weapon and his wits about him. The idea of staying in the saloon, like sitting ducks, was almost as crazy as this entire situation.

It was hard making sense of any of this. Just what had he gotten himself into?

The women threw on their coats. Jess gripped the screwdriver. Trinity, a bottle.

Eddie took a couple of tentative steps to the saloon entrance. He slowly dragged open the door, letting in a blast of the cutting wind. Then he craned his neck outside and glanced in both directions.

The howling blizzard stung his face.

The distant town square, identified from the map, seemed more appealing than the route leading into total darkness.

He looked back. "You guys ready?"

They both nodded.

"Let's stay quiet and keep our eyes peeled," Jess added.

Eddie headed out into the freezing conditions. He hunched against the wind, glancing in all directions. No lights were on in the general store or the bakery. As he trudged through the snow, closer to the square, the town's details became clear.

Four ornate streetlights cast creepy shadows across the surrounding buildings. Again, all looked closed for the night—if they'd ever been open in the first place. A giant Christmas tree had been erected in the center of the space. Several of its multicolored bulbs flickered, highlighting a small wooden newsstand.

A dark, retro merry-go-round sat on the other side of the tree. The red-and-white-striped drop rods, running from the platform to the crediting board, looked in great condition. The same went for the twenty white horses with flowing golden manes. And the painting on the circular wall that wrapped around the center pole.

At the far end of the square, the silhouette of a larger

building stood over everything else. But no lights were on inside.

Eddie shuddered and zipped his bomber jacket to the top.

The group stood close to one another, looking in all directions, taking in the bizarre abandoned town.

Once more, no cars in sight. No people. He had no idea what time it was.

"Over there," Trinity said, motioning her head to a nearby store. "There's a light behind the door."

They headed over to the single-story building. The sign above identified it as a cobbler's shop. Eddie carefully approached the door. From here, it looked like a small security light behind the panel of frosted glass. He moved across to the store's window and peered into the pitch black.

"Don't think anyone's here," he said.

"Try busting in," Trinity encouraged.

"You serious?"

"Why not?"

"Because I'm not a burglar."

"You think any of this shit is real?"

Eddie considered the question for a moment. Real or not, he didn't have much to lose. The thought of warmth and safety drove him on. Besides, it wouldn't be the first business he'd broken into, though there was no need to reveal his checkered history to the group.

He grabbed the door's brass knob and twisted.

Locked.

And the freezing metal stung his palm.

"Ah, to hell with it," he said.

Eddie took a short step back and slammed his heel against the lock.

A loud groan echoed around the town square.

The entire store frontage collapsed back, falling like a tree until it hammered against the ground. Wispy clouds of snow burst upward. The two buildings on either side remained standing, and both had walls. But this one . . . It was an even bigger fake than the saloon and had probably been put here for appearance.

They stared into the dark, snowy forest beyond.

"What the hell?" Trinity said. "This is getting weirder by the second."

Jess rapidly spun in the opposite direction, peering back toward the street.

"What is it?" Eddie said.

"I thought I heard something."

The three of them stood frozen by the collapsed frontage.

He raised his knife, straining to see through the terrible conditions. The last thing he expected to see was the old couple struggling out of the darkness for a confrontation. But he'd already figured that they weren't working alone.

Moments later, a figure emerged through the driving snow. Coming directly for them at a slow walk. A tall man. And he had what looked like a steel pipe in his right hand.

"Run!" Trinity yelled.

"Wait!" Eddie ordered. "Let's stay together."

Jess moved to his side. "He's right. Get behind me, Trinity."

Eddie braced, ready to meet the approaching man head-on. With violence, if necessary.

5

Jess tensed as they waited for the man to approach. Her body trembled from the cold. She stomped on the ground a few times to get her circulation moving. Eddie stood a couple of yards to her left, rocking on his heels. He seemed proactive, unafraid to make a move or stand his ground in the face of apparent danger.

As for Trinity Jackson? It had been harder to form an initial view of her capabilities. Jess guessed neither of them possessed her survival skills. And to be frank, she didn't quite trust either one. But like it or not, they were in this situation together.

The mysterious man shambled toward them, looking like an extra out of *The Walking Dead*. He passed through a streetlight's weak yellow glow, bringing him into focus for a moment when he was about forty feet away. It was hard to tell if he'd been injured or just moved this way as a form of intimidation. Slow, steady, and ominous. His business suit had been buttoned up, with the lapels raised.

One thing Jess was sure about, though. The man was clearly aware of the group—he was on a direct path toward the flattened storefront. Maybe he'd heard it collapse. Maybe he'd been watching them from the shadows, deciding when to strike.

"Who the fuck are you?" Eddie shouted. "Stay back."

The man shuffled forward a few more steps, then stopped in the ankle-deep snow. He just stood there, gazing at the group. An ice cloud blasted between them, shrouding him from view.

This was the time for the man to charge. If that was his intention.

Jess raised the screwdriver.

"I'm warning you," Eddie shouted. "Stay. Back."

When the cloud cleared, the man was still in the same place. He had his teeth clenched, left fist balled, and he hunched over a few inches.

Pain or anger?

A heartbeat later, the metal pole dropped from his hand. His upper body wavered, as if he'd downed a full bottle of liquor before heading out into the cold. Finally, he collapsed with a twist and thudded against the freezing ground.

Jess raced across the square toward him. For all she knew, the man might have already taken his final breath.

"Wait," Eddie called out. "We don't know who he is."

She skidded to a stop. "Did I know you before today? He's clearly injured."

"He has a pipe."

"We've got weapons too."

With more pressing matters at play, this conversation had to wait.

She pulled up a few feet from the body. He'd fallen onto his back, semiconscious and incoherently mumbling. He looked middle-aged, with a receding salt-and-pepper side part and a few wrinkles around his partially open eyes.

Jess breathed a sigh of relief and crouched next to the shivering man. She grabbed his steel pipe, tossed it away for safety, and leaned down for a closer look.

He definitely can't hurt me in this condition.

She patted his pockets, checking for a phone.

As expected, she found nothing.

He groaned. "Please . . . Help."

The man had bloodstains on his neck and the top of his dress shirt collar. She unbuttoned his jacket to examine the extent of his injuries.

Jess waved the other two over. "Get over here. Quick."

Eddie and Trinity held a hushed conversation—likely a quick argument about their limited options—and finally jogged over.

Something had sliced through the stranger's shirt and skin, creating three straight lacerations. Blood had soaked his clothing. Jess doubted he'd survive the night without medical attention. His wounds were almost certainly infected.

Trinity shot Eddie a nervous glance. "Where did you get that knife again?"

"The saloon."

"Really?"

"Are you out of your mind? You think I did this? For fuck's sake."

"Help . . ." the man gasped.

"What's your name?" Jess asked.

He mumbled something incoherently.

"We need to get him inside," Eddie said. "Gimme a hand, Jess. Trinity, you keep an eye out."

"Let's try the pharmacy," Jess replied. "It's our best shot."

They wrapped his arms around their shoulders and dragged him to his feet. The man tried to take stumbling steps, but he rested most of his weight on Jess's and Eddie's shoulders. She grunted as she helped him forward. The only saving grace was having the howling wind against their backs, pushing them toward their destination.

They hit Main Street in less than a minute and trudged along the middle of the road toward the nearby pharmacy.

Jess visually searched through every building window and down every alley.

Trinity stayed a few paces behind, evidently fearful of the group.

But who wouldn't be?

Slight indentations of footprints depressed the snow-covered ground. It was impossible to tell if they were theirs from earlier, or someone else's.

The group reached the pharmacy. A streetlight on the opposite side of the road cast a glare on its opaque window. Jess and Eddie leaned the man against the storefront. She kept his arm around her shoulder to avoid him collapsing again.

Eddie peered through the door. "At least this store is real."

He lowered the handle.

And the door creaked open.

"Wait a second," he said.

Eddie raised his knife and disappeared into the store. His footsteps echoed out onto the street as he searched the pharmacy. He eventually returned outside. "Looks like another old-school place, but there's some stuff on the shelves."

They helped the shivering man inside and propped him on a wicker chair. There was no heat in the building, but at least they had found temporary shelter from the elements.

The streetlight's glare provided enough light for the group to look around. The store had a long display case that doubled as a counter, packed with tiny boxes. On the wall behind, various-shaped bottles filled the shelves. It had the same old-style cash register as the saloon. A brass set of scales and measuring weights. And an array of antique measuring instruments.

Trinity, Eddie, and Jess started rummaging behind the counter, looking for any medicines of value. But every box they opened was empty. The bottles had no labels, just darkly colored liquids inside.

"They're all fakes," Trinity said, holding up an instrument.

Eddie sighed. "Just like everything else in this goddamned town."

Jess moved to the other side of the store and climbed a small set of wooden steps. She flipped open two overhead cupboards. A small cloud of dust dropped on her face. She closed her eyes for a moment and coughed. Reached inside and fished out gauze, a bandage roll, and a plastic bottle of pure alcohol.

"Guys," she said. "This'll do for now. At least we can bandage him up."

Eddie and Trinity stopped their search and headed back to the injured man. It appeared he'd come around a little, and he stared at them through bloodshot eyes.

"How you feeling, bro?" Eddie asked.

"Like shit." The man pressed his hand against his stomach. Hissed out breath through clenched teeth. "Some asshole jumped me."

"That sounds familiar," Trinity said. "What's your name?"

"Greg . . . Greg Fisher. Who are you? What's going on? Where am I?"

The group gave brief explanations of how they had been attacked. How they had woken up in this town. The strangeness of the bar and kitchen. Their decision to head outside. The store's false frontage in the town square. Then seeing him hobble through the blizzard.

Throughout this, Greg's expression changed from pain to fear. His eyes had widened, and he sat attentively, listening to their every word.

"How did they get you?" Trinity asked.

"The last thing I remember," Greg replied, still shaking from the frigid temperature inside the pharmacy, "I was leaving my house to meet potential investors. It was a big deal, you know? A once-in-a-lifetime opportunity. Now that's probably all up in smoke. Anyway, that's when I was assaulted."

"I meant how."

"Oh, I see. I was walking to my car, getting keys out of my pocket. There's a tree next to my driveway. A pink flowering dogwood that blooms for four weeks every spring. It's beautiful. Cars slow down to look—"

"How?" she demanded.

He returned her scowl while slowly shaking his head. "I'm getting there."

Greg had gone from apparently semiconscious to "too much information" in a matter of minutes. Sure, he had injuries that looked ugly, but it made Jess wonder if he was playing with them. Acting weak as a ruse. Testing to see if they were his abductors while he gained strength to act on his real intentions.

"Someone in black clothes and a balaclava jumped out from behind a tree. They moved fast. Slashed me three times across the stomach. I swung my briefcase at their head but missed. The damned thing flew open, sending my files across the front lawn." Greg shook his head again. "Anyway, the momentum of the swing turned me around. Before I could react, I think they stuck a needle in my neck. Then I woke up under the awning of an old store."

"The exact same thing happened to me," Eddie said. "The problem is establishing where we are, because I'm sure as hell that this isn't 1936. And how to get out of this fake living hell."

A small light winked in Jess's peripheral vision. She looked toward the far end of the pharmacy. A dome camera had been attached to the ceiling, and its red light only meant one thing.

"Not everything's fake. Look," she said. "We're being watched."

6

Eddie stormed to the back of the room, his eyes narrowed in anger. His career choice had taught him how to spot and avoid cameras. He'd thought he was streetwise and could see almost anything coming. Anyone observing him. However, this evening had transformed into his darkest night. A situation beyond any previous experience.

He stopped beneath the device, peering upward, imagining the callous old couple watching his every move from the safety and warmth of their living room.

"What the hell do you want from us?" he shouted, his breath fogging in the air.

The uncaring lens simply stared back at him.

Trinity moved to his side and yelled, "What twisted shit is this? Who are you?"

Again, nothing but a solid glare from the red pinhead light.

Eddie vaulted onto the counter. He grimaced from the pain in his cold, stiff limbs. He reached up, grabbed the camera, and slipped it out of the mount.

The device had no wires. He opened the back and flipped out two batteries. Then he smashed the camera on the ground.

"Quiet!" Trinity hissed.

"It's a bit late for that, don't you think?"

Jess helped the limping Greg to the back of store, though he didn't require much assistance. The injured man had grown visibly stronger during the last half hour, arousing Eddie's suspicion. All of them stared at the smashed camera parts, probably going over the implications of the discovery.

In his mind's eye, the old couple had just witnessed their screen going from footage of the store to a static hiss.

"More evidence that someone is around," Greg murmured.

Trinity tutted. "We're the only evidence you need. How else do you think we got here?"

"I meant *close* by."

"Don't forget the record player and the lamps in the saloon," Eddie added. "They are close by indeed, likely watching our every move. We're trapped in a goddamn zoo." He gazed out the window at the dimly lit street. "How are you feeling, Greg?"

"Honestly, best day of my life."

"Cut the sarcasm. I meant, do you have enough strength to head back out?"

"Head back out?" Greg retorted, looking at the storm raging outside the door. "You guys are not listening to me . . . I use similar cameras at home. They only have a range of a few hundred feet. Isn't it better to hole up in here to defend—"

"We can't stay here," Jess said firmly. "This building has no heat, no real supplies. We stay here, we freeze before sunrise."

Greg looked at her skeptically.

"Look," Jess continued, "we know we're being watched. We need to accept that something bizarre and dark has happened. No, *is* happening. Someone is clearly close by who means you harm. Our only choice is to escape when the sun rises. But for now, we've got to shelter up somewhere warm and dry, where we can defend ourselves from . . . whatever this all is."

Trinity and Greg glared at Jess. Neither of them struck Eddie as people who liked taking orders. But regardless of their thoughts, the clarity of Jess's words resonated in his mind, and brought back a flash of memory.

Maybe it was the directness of Jess's statement. Or her assertiveness, or confidence. Whatever it was, for a fleeting moment, Jess reminded Eddie of his ex from so long ago. The one that got away.

More accurately, the one that *ran* away when Eddie refused to give up being a damned thief. If he had the opportunity to live his life again, he would have chosen differently in that moment. Back then, he had let a potentially great life slip through his fingers. They'd even talked about marriage and kids. For a second, it made him feel even more hollow.

But that didn't matter right now.

Eddie nodded his head at the group. He jumped off the counter and his boots slammed against the ground. "Jess is right. We push on and find someplace warm until sunrise. Everyone stay close. We're stronger together."

"Hold on a sec, man," Greg said. "Where do we go?"

"Let's figure that out as we move."

Greg let out an exasperated sigh. "Fine. Okay."

Eddie turned to Trinity. "Ready to head out again?"

"I suppose, yes."

As the group walked to the front of the pharmacy, Eddie looked at each one of them in turn. Jess seemed focused on the task ahead. Brow furrowed, screwdriver in hand, her eyes fixed on the street. She'd had a firm grasp on the situation throughout.

Trinity was wild-eyed and skittish.

Greg returned a cynical glare . . . He was harder to read, but everyone appeared stricken in their own way. And freezing. Once they stepped outside, hypothermia would accelerate quickly. They had to move fast.

Eddie creaked open the door and scanned in both directions. Their previous footprints were still partially visible in the snow, though quickly disappearing in the fresh layers of snow.

He glanced over his shoulder one more time. "I say we head back through town. Check out the big building on the far side of the square."

Eddie extended his knife and headed back out into the cutting wind. He leaned forward, bracing against the weather, prepared to react. Jess walked by his side, checking out the storefronts on either side of the road.

The streetlights cast everyone's elongated shadow on the ground, allowing Eddie to keep an eye on the two who followed a few steps behind. Well, specifically Greg. There was something about the guy that had raised a red flag.

Exactly what kind of flag, he had no concrete idea. Despite Greg's injuries, he'd come across as the least trustworthy. Like a used car salesman trying to sell a customer a lemon.

The group headed past the flickering bulbs on the large Christmas tree, the collapsed storefront, and the static merry-go-round. The dark silhouettes of the buildings loomed on the opposite side of the square.

Each crunching footstep in the snow sounded too loud for comfort. Eddie peered at the black windows, searching for any signs of movement. He had no doubt in his mind that they were being watched. And he suspected that the group wouldn't be allowed to simply walk out of this fake town. Not when so much effort had been involved to get them here in the first place.

"What are you doing?" Trinity barked.

Eddie spun to face the two behind.

Greg kicked his feet around in the snow, close to the place

where he'd earlier collapsed. Eventually, he hit something solid and retrieved the metal pipe he had dropped.

Jess and Eddie exchanged a quick glance. Her concerned look mirrored his thoughts, but now wasn't the right time to have this discussion.

They reached within a few footsteps of the largest building in town, a three-story wooden structure that had been painted white. Stairs led up to a set of double doors. A snow-covered sign sat at the front. Eddie swept his arm across it, revealing fancy lettering spelling out the words:

Old Forge Town Hall

Jess strode up the groaning stairs toward the doors. She grabbed a handle and slowly hauled the right one open.

Eddie joined her at the entrance, staring into the dark, cavernous space. The roof was only half-finished, with naked beams stretching across the ceiling. Snow had settled on the dirt ground inside the structure.

"Fuck," he exclaimed.

"What's inside?" Trinity asked from the bottom of the steps.

"Nothing. It's just an empty shell. See for yourself."

Trinity and Greg climbed the steps and peered through the door.

"What the hell is going on?" Trinity said, baffled. "What now?"

"We keep going," Eddie replied.

The group headed back down the steps and stood in the square.

Eddie gazed in all directions. His entire body trembled. The group needed to find somewhere warm soon.

For a fleeting moment, he caught sight of a faint light through the blizzard. It came from outside the square.

Then again. A brief twinkle.

"Guys," he whispered. "Over there."

They watched for a few seconds, straining to see through the whipping snow.

"Anyone remember what that building was on the map?" Trinity asked.

Jess shrugged. "I think it was a church. I'm not sure."

Eddie's feet and hands had gone completely numb. With their options severely limited, the group had to press forward and explore. He set off at a steady walk, heart racing, heading for the source of the light.

This time, nobody argued about their direction of travel.

The light became brighter as they left the square and soon became a solid glow. Jess had been right. A two-story church had a steeple that led down to a large wooden door. It lay ajar, with a thin spear of light punching out into the darkness.

Eddie extended a flat palm, gesturing the others to wait.

He crept forward on his own. A picket fence surrounded the church's small grounds. Neat rows of gravestones jutted from the snow.

Within a few feet of the door, he stopped.

Raised his knife in alarm.

Shouting came from inside the church.

Two men, arguing, loudly.

Something crashed inside, sounding like a collection plate rattling across a stone floor. The rest of the group had ignored Eddie's instruction and now stood by his side. He opened the door a few more inches and craned his head inside.

Candles lit the entire church from the altar to the entrance. A lifesaving cocoon of warmth enveloped the group, courtesy of a lit wood furnace in the far corner of the building.

Inside, two men wrestled between a row of pews, wildly throwing punches and trading insults, completely unaware of their new audience. One was large and overweight, wearing a blue tracksuit. The other was lean, dressed in black cargo pants and a sweater.

"They could've been forcibly taken here," Jess whispered from behind, "just like us."

Her comment made sense. That being said, they could also be their captors. Or at least one of them, anyway.

Eddie pushed into the church and the group followed behind.

"Hey!" he shouted. "Stop fighting. Right now!"

Whether they heard him or not, the men continued their desperate battle.

Eddie moved deeper into the church, knife held forward. "I said stop!"

Once again, it wasn't enough to break their focus.

Greg hustled around Eddie. He slammed his metal pipe against a pew, sending a loud metallic thud reverberating around the church.

The fighters instantly jumped at the sound and backed away from each other.

The lean man in black quickly slipped into the darkness by the side of the pulpit.

The larger guy in the tracksuit stared at the group, sucking in deep breaths. He pointed toward the shadows. "That motherfucker jumped me."

His response sounded genuine and frantic.

Before Eddie had a chance to reply, the church's side door flew open, and the lean man raced out into the night.

7

ind howled through the open side door, blowing out a few of the candles. Eddie took a moment to process what he had just witnessed. The man in the tracksuit claimed he was jumped. The other fled without saying a word.

The question of which one looked the most innocent seemed clear, though Eddie was taking nothing for granted.

However, it also meant the group might be facing only one enemy . . . for now. And from what Eddie had seen, neither of the two fighters had used any weapons.

"Keep an eye on him," Eddie yelled, pointing his knife at Tracksuit.

He raced through the church, passing several neat rows of pews, and reached the door. The lean man had disappeared into the shroud of the blizzard outside. Footprints in the snow led back toward town.

Eddie dragged the door shut and locked the dead bolt.

Back in the center of the room, Trinity, Greg, and Jess had kept their distance from the remaining fighter.

"Where the fuck am I?" Tracksuit shouted.

The confusion written across his face—and his ill-suited clothing for the weather outside—made him look like another person who had been pulled into this living hell against his will.

Eddie tentatively approached.

"Back off," Tracksuit yelled.

"We're not here to hurt you," Eddie said.

The man in the tracksuit laughed. "I'd like to see you try, dick."

Eddie sized the man up and down. He wasn't wrong. The guy was probably fifty pounds heavier than him, if not more. It wouldn't be much of a fight.

"Look," Eddie said. "Each one of us was kidnapped."

"Oh yeah? Then what's with the knife, bro?"

"Protection."

"From who?"

"We've got no idea," Trinity called out.

Tracksuit peered around the church while backing toward the altar. He had all the hallmarks of a typical guy that Eddie used to run with in the old neighborhood. Bling, ink, a buzz cut, stubble. The guy was built like a brick shithouse. The kind of person you wanted on your side, but you'd tell your kids to avoid.

Eddie placed his knife on a pew and held his hands up non-threateningly. "Did you wake up here?"

"I came to with that asshole's hands around my neck."

"Any idea who he was?"

"No." He glanced at the dark stained-glass windows. "Where are we? And don't just say a church."

"A deserted town. Don't know where. We all woke up here too."

"You shitting me?"

The rest of the group moved to Eddie's side.

"Look at the state of us," Jess said. "Does it look like he's kidding?"

Tracksuit gave the group a suspicious glare. "You know what it looks like to me? Four people, all tooled up," he said, pointing at their makeshift weapons. "Aw man, fuck this. Fuck all y'all. I'll take my chances on my own."

The man headed along the central walkway. He skirted everyone while keeping a close eye on them.

"I wouldn't leave if I were you," Jess said.

"She's right," Eddie shouted. "You don't know what you're facing."

"And this is the only building we've found with heat," Jess added, pointing to the furnace that was slowly dying out in the corner.

The man in the tracksuit stopped a few yards from the front door. He slowly turned, with a scowling look on his face.

"Just listen for two minutes, then make up your mind. My name is Jess. This is Trinity, Eddie, and Greg."

The man slowly nodded his head. "All right, I'll play. The name is Tank. You've got two minutes to explain all this shit."

He checked his wrist. His eyes widened as he patted his pockets. "That motherfucker stole all my shit."

"All of us have been robbed," Eddie said. "Listen up for a minute."

Everyone briefly told Tank their own story. The last thing they remembered. How they woke up in the artificial town. The fake telephone in the saloon. The absence of people and vehicles. The security camera. The bone-chilling conditions outside. Finally, coming across the church and its lifesaving heat, among other things.

Tank gazed at the ground in thought. He leaned out of the front door for a few seconds, then retreated into the church. "Okay, this definitely isn't Utica."

"You got that right," Eddie said. "What's the last thing you remember?"

"I was in the alley alongside the bar, waiting to do a deal with my buyer—"

Greg snorted. "A drug deal."

"Shut the hell up, bitch. We're both in the same boat. Someone hit me from behind with a needle. Next thing, I'm in this church with a guy trying to choke me out."

"Was it the same guy?" Trinity asked.

"I'm not sure. Maybe. Maybe he's on the same team as that old couple that jumped you," Tank said to Eddie.

"Ha." Greg laughed. "This is all insane."

Tank took a long look at Greg, stepping toward him. "Wait a second. I know you."

Greg shook his head. "I seriously doubt it, buddy."

"Yeah, I do," Tank insisted. "You're that douchebag who ripped off pensioners for thousands."

"That's bullshit, man."

"Yeah, I remember seeing it on TV. Seeing a photo of your smug ass. I remember telling my buddy that your last name shoulda been Shark instead of . . . what was it again . . . Fish?"

"Fisher," Eddie said.

"That's right. Greg Fisher."

Greg swallowed hard. "I didn't scam anyone out of anything. It was a series of wrong investments. That's all."

"Bro, you actually believe your own shit?" Tank burst out laughing. "Is that what you call your Ponzi scheme? 'A series of wrong investments'? How many grandmothers did you scam out of their life savings again?"

"Fuck off, man," Greg shot back. "At least I'm not some two-bit drug dealer."

Tank took a step toward Greg, clenching his fists. It appeared

YOU BETTER WATCH OUT

he was about to start another fight, and likely hammer the apparent snake oil salesman into next week.

Eddie stepped between them before the church witnessed more flying punches.

"Let's cool it, guys. We're not enemies here."

"Maybe not," Jess said. "But their stories might be a clue."

"What do you mean?"

"Maybe the people that kidnapped us want payback. It could be a local street gang, maybe vigilantes or something?"

Tank nodded slowly, understanding. "I get what you're saying. Given my . . . career path, and the douchebag over here, maybe someone is looking for some revenge."

"The logic tracks," Eddie replied.

"Yeah, but one thing doesn't. If that's the case, I know why I'm here, and I know why the Shark is here. So, the question is, why are the rest of *you* here?"

Jess, Trinity, and Eddie looked at each other in silence. Once again, the last thing he wanted to admit was that he'd tried to steal from an old couple after helping them to the safety of a dark parking lot. Even though his crime appeared mild compared with the other two men's. Relatively speaking.

"Well?" Tank pressed.

"I haven't done anything wrong," Trinity said.

"Same," Jess added.

"Look, this doesn't matter right now," Eddie said.

"Fuck yeah, it matters," Tank shot back. "We've all been kidnapped. Some dude just tried to kill me. He might be on his way back to finish the job right now. I wanna know why."

"You're right. He might be on his way back. Which is why we need to barricade these doors *now*. Everything else can wait."

"True," Jess chimed in. "We've got shelter; we've got warmth in this church. Now, it's time for our safety. We barricade the entrances using the pews. Then, we head out at sunrise to find our way out of this town."

Eddie nodded at Jess, breathing a sigh of relief that he hadn't been forced to admit his sins for all to hear. Although if there was one place to confess your sins, it was in church.

Sure, he had made plenty of shit choices in his life—and one especially bad choice that had haunted him ever since—but he was planning on turning it all around.

Tank shook his head, backing down for now. He moved to the nearest wooden pew and lifted one end of it. "All right, assholes. Someone gimme a hand."

8

Jess growled as she lifted the last pew into place. The warmth of the church and the work had given her a welcome boost. Eddie and Trinity had helped pile six of the benches against the front entrance. Tank the dealer and Greg the swindler—the two most unpredictable of the group in Jess's mind—had done the same to secure the side door.

Jess's thoughts turned to the shadowy figure that fled the church earlier tonight. Was he attacking Tank, or was he a confused victim of circumstance like the rest of them? Was he dangerous? Would he return?

One thing was certain—if he did return, he'd have little chance of reentering the church. It was beginning to look like the barricade from *Les Misérables*.

With the final pew in defensive position, the group's attention turned toward the furnace in the corner, which was nearly extinguished. They instinctively huddled around the remaining warmth, hands outstretched.

"Let's get some more heat into this place, or it's gonna get real cold real quick," Eddie said, moving over to a pile of firewood next to the furnace. "We're gonna need more than this."

"Agreed," Jess replied. "Let's look for anything and everything we can use to stoke the fire once we toss these logs in."

"I got an idea," Tank said. "Why don't we burn some of Greg's stock tips? I'm sure they'll go right up in flames."

Greg stared into Tank's eyes, unflinching. His face twisted

into a look of disgust. He lunged toward the much larger man in anger and grabbed him by his tracksuit.

With one powerful swipe, Tank knocked Greg to the ground like a rag doll.

"You wanna go? Let's go!" he shouted over the sketchy salesman.

Without skipping a beat, Eddie jumped between them, once again separating the two before things got out of hand.

"Knock it off!" Jess bellowed. "We've got enough problems right now, and don't need this shit."

She couldn't believe how much these guys were acting like overgrown children. The last thing she wanted was for events to spiral out of control. She needed calm and logic to dictate the group's every move. Reasoning in the face of adversity.

"Tank," she said, "go check out the rest of the church with Trinity and Eddie. Greg and I will get the fire back up and running."

Eddie placed a hand on Tank's shoulder. "Come on, buddy. Let's see if we can find any supplies—water, food, anything."

The other three headed away, leaving Jess alone with an out-of-breath Greg.

Out of everyone in the group, she sensed Eddie was the one who would help her steer things in the right direction. He had registered their dilemma and need for immediate survival the fastest. In this messed-up, enclosed world, she considered him her best asset.

"All right, how do you wanna get this thing stoked?" Greg asked, brushing himself off.

"Find some kindling. Paper. Cloth. Twigs. Anything that's easy to light."

He stood to face her. "You got it."

"And Greg, can you do me a small favor?"

Greg let out a long sigh. "I get it. Tank and I put our differences aside until we get outta this frozen shithole."

Jess gave him a thin smile. "Something like that. None of us know what the hell is happening. But I do know killing each other isn't the solution."

Greg nodded. "How do you keep so calm?"

"Someone has to keep a cool head, right?"

Jess tossed a piece of firewood into the furnace.

Greg headed toward the altar, scanning the room for flammable kindling.

A loud groan broke the quiet, echoing around the walls. Greg stopped mid-stride, staring toward the far end of the church.

Trinity had opened the large wooden door to a back room. Old hinges screeched. Eddie and Tank slowly entered with candles in one hand, weapons in the other, exploring the room.

"What's in there?" Jess called out.

"Looks like the church's vestry," Eddie shouted back. "There's a couple of closets, a desk, and some drawers. Give us a second."

Greg returned to the furnace with a tattered, leather-bound Bible. He flipped it open. "You think this'll work?"

"Well, you might go to hell for it . . ."

"I'm already there," he said dryly.

Greg tore out bunched pages, scrunched them, and tossed each one into the furnace. The hot embers immediately ignited the paper and bright yellow flames erupted inside.

Soon, the pieces of wood gave off a healthy crackle. Jess fed more of the paper inside until the fire took hold. By the time the others came back from the office, welcoming heat was waiting to warm their bodies.

Eddie and Trinity stood near the furnace, holding their hands close to its metal sides. They had managed to find a couple of white blankets and a kerosene lamp. Tank had stayed a few steps away, concealing something behind his back. The smug look on his face suggested it was something worth discovering.

"Find anything useful?" Jess asked the group.

"Just blankets," Eddie said. "The church looks . . . unused, like every damn thing in this town."

Greg gave Tank an icy stare. "What are *you* hiding?"

Tank flamboyantly produced a dusty green bottle. "Holy wine, bitches. *You* get warmth your way. *I'll* get mine from the good Lord."

"I don't think you should drink that . . ." Jess said.

"Don't worry, little lady. I'll share with you, promise." Tank wiped dust away from the label. "Besides, the bottle is sealed. California 2021 merlot. Praise Jesus."

"Buddy, Jess is right," Eddie implored. "We should avoid—"

"Fuck off, bro."

Tank screwed off the cap and tossed it over his shoulder. The small piece of aluminum bounced a few times, coming to a stop by the altar's steps.

Jess's heart hammered against her chest. She understood that this was one situation where she couldn't get in the way, regardless of the stupid decision that was about to be carried out.

Anyone with half a brain, considering their situation, would use sound logic to dictate their every move. Everyone had to act with extreme caution at all turns.

Tank's irrational behavior disturbed her. It threw things out of their natural order. He made things less predictable. Less plannable. He made others more prone to make wild decisions. And that led to stupid calls.

Who woulda thought a drug dealer would be prone to irrational decisions, she thought.

In short, he had rapidly proved to be the group's biggest liability.

Tank held the wine bottle close to his lips. "Bon appétit, bitches."

He took three rapid gulps with a shit-eating grin on his face.

A split second later, the grin faded and his entire body jerked.

The bottle dropped from his hand and shattered on the stone floor, scattering wine and fragments of glass.

Liquid sprayed from Tank's mouth as he let out a garbled, bloodcurdling roar.

Everyone stood paralyzed, confused by the sight.

Tank violently clamped his hands around his jaw, in agonizing pain. The veins in his neck throbbed. His eyes bulged in complete shock at what was happening. A moment later, he collapsed backward and his shoulders slammed against the stone floor.

Jess went to take a step forward, but paused.

Tank's roar turned into a sporadic, gargling wheeze.

Circular red burn marks spontaneously appeared around his throat.

Blood pooled out from under him. His shoulders repeatedly jolted up and crashed back down. It appeared as if the holy wine had given him an almighty electric shock, but that wasn't the case.

Jess lunged forward and straddled Tank. She ripped open his tracksuit, trying to see what was suddenly happening to his body.

The same circular red markings had appeared on the upper part of his chest and continued blooming, like a fast-spreading disease. Parts of his skin bubbled, then popped, releasing thin wisps of smoke each time they burst.

Trinity screamed until her lungs emptied. Greg and Eddie backed away to avoid the blood and whatever substance Tank had greedily consumed.

Jess stared into Tank's eyes. He returned a look of pure terror for a few moments, until his face relaxed and he vacantly stared at the church's vaulted ceiling toward the heavens above.

It had only taken seconds from his first drink to his last breath.

Nobody could have saved him.

Jess let out a shuddering breath.

Silence filled the church. Tank's death had been self-inflicted, brutal, and fast. A horrific sight for even the darkest of people.

His legs twitched beneath Jess for a terrifying moment, until finally, he lay motionless.

Jess scrambled away from the corpse and crashed into the closest pew. She peered at his lifeless remains, then checked her hands to make sure none of the liquid had burned her own skin.

"What the fuck," Eddie breathed. He leaned over a pool of the bubbling liquid on the church's floor. He pushed a torn-out page from the Book of Revelations into the liquid with his foot, and almost instantly, the paper dissolved into nothing.

"Acid," Eddie said in horror. "He just drank pure acid . . ."

9

ess watched as Trinity sank to her knees. She cupped a hand over Trinity's mouth, but it didn't hide or reduce the sound of her hyperventilation.

Eddie moved across and wrapped a comforting arm around Trinity. They both looked more terrified than when Jess had first seen them in the saloon's kitchen. It was an understandable reaction. But it was the world they were living in right now, and Tank had made and paid for his bad decision.

For the next few minutes, most of the group remained silent, seemingly unable to find the right words to understand what had happened. And the consequences.

Eventually, Greg murmured, "What a fucking idiot."

"Excuse me?" Trinity replied.

"You heard me. Dumbass went and got himself killed. We all said not to drink that."

"Funny, Greg," Eddie said. "I remember Jess saying that. I remember myself saying that. But I don't remember you saying jack shit to stop him."

"Whatever, man. He was a piece of shit anyway."

Eddie shook his head in disbelief.

Jess headed over to the blankets. She grabbed the corners of one and snapped it open, sending out a small dust cloud.

"What are you doing?" Greg asked cynically.

"I'm covering his body. Or do you wanna keep looking at it?"

"Save the blankets for the living. He doesn't need them anymore."

"You're a real dick, Greg," Eddie said. He rose from Trinity's side and grabbed the other end of the blanket. "We still need to get warm and dry off. I say we stay here until dawn, but let's be very careful what we touch."

"Totally agree," Jess replied.

"For all we know, this whole place is a trap. Who knows what other nasty surprises are waiting for us outside."

"What if they come for us?" Trinity asked in a shaky voice.

"Then we fight them with everything we've got."

They draped the blanket over Tank's body. Patches of blood slowly appeared on the surface. His left arm remained uncovered, and his milky white hand had contorted into an unnatural shape. Eddie nudged it underneath the blanket with his boot.

Trinity whimpered. "Oh my God."

But there was no divine spirit between these four walls.

Tank had no savior.

His prayers had received a gruesome answer.

The long night had just gotten a whole lot longer. Though each passing hour would bring a new day. A route away from the darkness. And opportunities for Jess to ensure she wouldn't end up dead.

10

The glow from the furnace illuminated everyone's faces as they lay around the fire, covered in blankets on the floor. It had been quiet and warm, but the first signs of daylight told Eddie that things were about to change.

The darkness behind the stained-glass windows had turned to a paler shade, in keeping with the muffled sound of morning songbirds. The wind had also stopped blasting against the side of the church. A promising sign, albeit a small one.

The group had managed to keep the fire going throughout the night by smashing up a wooden pew and using it as fuel. They'd also briefly opened the church's side door and scooped up some snow. Melted it on the collection plate to quench their thirst. No one dared touch any of the various bottles in the vestry.

Still, it had been a painful few hours. Infinitely worse than being locked up with a bunch of violent drunks in a cell, which Eddie had done more than a few times in his life.

As more time passed since Tank's death, Trinity regained her old attitude: frowning, finger-pointing, repeatedly questioning the plan. Eddie guessed the enormity of their plight had finally sunk in, and she desperately wanted out now.

But nobody had the answer to that need.

Greg had been Greg: an Olympic-sized pain in the ass. He'd sat around bitching about Tank's drug dealing and speculating over Eddie's, Trinity's, and Jess's histories. His wild nutjob theories included them being part of the same deadly cult, or that they'd contaminated the water supply in Syracuse, and he asked weird questions about their family trees. He wouldn't buy for a second that they weren't here for smaller crimes than his own scheme. Everyone denied it or, like Eddie, stayed tight-lipped.

But something else had been playing on Eddie's mind.

"There has to be a road out of here," he said to the group. "Otherwise, how did they bring in the raw materials to build a duplicate of Old Forge from back in the day?"

"Nobody is carrying a merry-go-round through a forest," Jess added.

"Precisely right," Eddie agreed.

Greg shrugged. "But don't you think it's possible we're in some kind of abandoned ghost town or something?"

"You saw those beams in the town hall. The roof looks like it's currently under construction. The saloon smelt of new timber, too. I'm not saying that makes it brand-new, but this town can't be more than a few years old."

"Okay, but why does this place even exist then?" Trinity asked.

Eddie considered the question. "Well, all this wasn't built just to kill Tank. That's for sure."

Jess nodded in agreement. "So we find the route out. Track the road from a safe distance and see where it leads. Any suggestions where to start?"

Eddie replayed the night's events in his mind. Every direction looked like it was surrounded by forest, but it was impossible to be certain because of the blizzard. "Let's head past the saloon and check out the other end of town."

"Are you sure?" Trinity said. "That way looked like a dead end to me."

"And it very well may be. Or maybe that's what they want

us to believe. The one thing I want to avoid, though, is hiking to the middle of nowhere and being caught in another blizzard. That'll guarantee we go the same way as Tank."

"Not *quite* the same way," Greg said sarcastically.

Eddie ignored the comment. "The sun is rising. We bundle up and head out, right? We need to stick together. We need to stay quiet. Deal with any threats collectively. Put an end to this madness."

Jess and Trinity nodded along to his words.

Eddie took a last glimpse of Tank's covered body. Considered what he was about to face. Their abductors had no problem indirectly killing people. That said, the group had been left alone since the lean man had bolted out of the church.

The best case was that everyone had been put here to teach them a harsh lesson. And Tank had paid the ultimate price, never learning from his mistakes. This was Eddie's best and faintest hope.

The worst case? Death.

He expected that during this next make-or-break dash through the town, everything would become clear. They'd either escape to real civilization . . . or it would be a fight to the end. Without food and with the constant prospect of imminent danger, everyone had little choice but to head out.

That was the point, though.

Their captors surely realized this, which probably meant they had also anticipated the group's next move and had already planned ahead. Which meant big trouble.

Eddie led the group toward the front of the church, propelled by nervous energy. They hauled away the pews without saying a word. Eddie internally braced himself. Took a deep breath and opened the door.

A few clouds hung in the dark blue sky, and the sun's orange glow brightened the horizon. A gust of wind passed through the town square and main street—*the only street*—of Old Forge, blowing mists of snow off building roofs.

No footprints covered the ground between the church and the main part of town. And no detectable sounds rose above the chorus of birds. If anything, Old Forge looked benign, though he felt sure this wouldn't last long.

The shadowy figure who fought with Tank was somewhere out there. Watching from a dark window. Waiting for the right opportunity. Eddie felt sure about that. But he also had confidence in his own ability when it came to a fight.

Everyone stepped out into the bitter morning air, weapons raised.

"Keep your eyes peeled," Jess said.

"You don't need to tell me that," Greg snapped back.

Eddie headed for the Christmas tree at the near end of the square.

The snow came up to his shins as he waded forward, searching in all directions for anything suspicious. The sheer height of the snowdrifts made walking through the town utterly exhausting.

Trinity and Jess flanked him as they hit the end of the main street.

With natural light improving by the minute, it allowed Eddie a chance to pick out more details. Christmas decorations had been attached above each lamppost. Some of the stores' awnings sagged under the weight of the snow, but all—a hardware store, a bakery with what looked like plastic bread behind the window, an inn at the end of the street with posts outside to tether nonexistent horses—had immaculately painted signage above.

He shivered as he passed the saloon.

It would've taken a strong person to carry a 180-pound unconscious body through a forest. It was a tough job for two people. No, they must have brought him here in a vehicle. Which meant there was a way out.

But he couldn't remember seeing any tire tracks. Then again, the blizzard would have covered them fast.

Jess leaned toward him. "So far, so good."

"We've still got a long way to go."

They were heading along the street toward him.

First two appeared, then two more.

He crouched behind a bedroom window on the first floor of the inn. Backed up a few more inches behind the stale-smelling drapes. Lowered his breathing to minimize the amount of breath clouding in the air. His black clothes blended well with the dark interior.

They wouldn't see him.

His experience of stalking prey put him at a massive advantage.

This time was different, though. He'd shadow them. Allow them to make errors. Benefit from their flawed judgment. Then only reveal himself when the time was right. Today was all about timing.

He glanced down at the heavy axe in his right hand. Its blade was razor-sharp. The weight felt good. One hefty swing would take out even the most formidable enemy.

Four people had left the church and headed his way. Like

lambs to the slaughter. Methodically yet stupidly walking past the stores that contained nothing useful, checking out every window as they closed on the inn.

The men were armed with a pipe and a knife, the women with what looked like tools. He wondered about this ragtag crew's capability. How close-knit they had become overnight. If a selfish person or a betrayer had infested their ranks.

It seemed likely, given the typical human condition. Luckily for him, he operated outside of those circles. He had the ability to zoom out of life and view it from a godlike vantage point.

Each of these fools had stood like a deer in headlights, allowing him to escape without a single question. No effort to hinder his escape. They were hardly the actions of a proactive and dynamic crew. And he knew they couldn't stay in the church forever. That's how normal people rolled. And predictably, they had headed in his direction.

He frowned when it became apparent the fat guy in the tracksuit wasn't there. Maybe he'd been killed. It didn't matter. If so, someone had simply finished his job. The only shame in that was that he hadn't been able to witness the idiot's death.

The group moved level with the inn, still oblivious to the hungry eyes that tracked their every move. They were nothing more than puppets on strings, allowing a greater force to dictate their every move.

A bolt of sexual excitement shot through his body.

His breathing became staccato.

He pursed his lips.

Images of his last victim rushed to the front of his mind. How the teenage girl had screamed and fought against him. Hammered her fists against his chest. How she'd put up a futile fight against his overwhelming strength and urge. He'd loved every second.

The fact that he was aroused came as no surprise.

Thrills came in many forms, but he'd always found the biggest turn-on was power—especially over people.

The four directly below the window were at his mercy.

They would do his bidding.

And if everything panned out how he expected—and he saw no reason to doubt himself—he would be the last man standing in this replica of Old Forge.

11

E ddie headed past the last two stores on either side of the
street. Both dark and dismal without any signs of light,
mirroring his future prospects. Ahead, the evergreen forest's canopy protected a small section of the cobblestones, but
the Main Street road stopped abruptly a few yards beyond the
tree line. He visually searched for a route to salvation. Any hint
of a trail between the tightly packed spruce, firs, and tamaracks
that enveloped the entire town.

But he found no obvious way out.

The road just ended in the densely packed forest.

He shook his head at the impossibility. The thought of a
merry-go-round being physically carried here was utterly ridic-
ulous. It would have needed a small army. Eddie turned to the
others, exasperated.

"Okay, this is a dead end. Let's go for plan B. We head around
the perimeter of the town. See if we can find a damned road or
path out of here."

For the next twenty minutes, the group struggled through
the snow, skirting the back of the buildings around the edge of
the town. Eddie's boots had been made with fashion in mind
and were already soaked through. His toes had begun to numb
again, but he pressed on at a good pace, the best way of keeping
warm.

Greg and Trinity quietly cursed when they lost their balance, stumbling over snow-covered rocks and branches. For the

first time, Eddie wondered if "safety in numbers" was actually the best approach.

Do Greg and Trinity increase or decrease my chances of surviving? He wasn't sure.

To his right, Jess stayed silent and stoic. Grim-faced and determined. He caught her eye and received a firm nod of approval. If this was a demented competition, like a survival of the fittest or smartest, she was his main rival.

But her calmness and clarity also boosted his chances of freedom.

Focus, he told himself. *These people are not the ones intending harm.*

For the moment, at least. He had lost the ability to trust anyone a very long time ago, due to tragic circumstances, and that had suited him well in life.

Eddie led everyone in single file, behind the stores, church, and square. The tree line lay roughly fifty yards from the buildings. This meant the perfectly contoured cutout of the forest was too perfect to be natural. Clearing enough trees to create the space for the town was a massive job, certainly beyond the capabilities of the old couple that had kidnapped him yesterday.

Hell, this would be a difficult job for an entire team of people with heavy equipment. For a hot second, he considered if this was some twisted reality show, before his memory of Tank's horrific fate in the church demolished that idea.

Eddie searched the ground, looking for any clues. All footprints from last night had vanished. The flattened frontage of the cobbler's store had been buried. Eventually, and maddeningly, they circumnavigated the town and arrived back at the same spot at the end of the street.

"What the fuck," Greg said to no one in particular.

Eddie gazed down Main Street. Sunlight glinted off icicles that hung from store signs. In the distance, the brightness of the morning had dulled the glow of the Christmas tree bulbs.

"So much for a way in or out," Greg said, shivering. "I knew this was a stupid idea."

"We had to try," Jess replied.

"We failed, obviously."

Anger flared inside Eddie. "Remind me, what was your plan again, Greg? Right, you didn't have one, dick."

Greg turned away, tutting.

"Okay, let's think about this," Jess said. "We're surrounded on all sides by the forest. All the trees are at least a hundred feet tall. Which means they've been here for years, maybe a century or more. So, how did this town get built?"

"No shit," Trinity scoffed.

"That doesn't answer my question, Trinity. Eddie's right, there's *got* to be a road somewhere and we're just missing it. We need to keep looking."

"Hey, here's an idea," Greg said. "Let's just use Google Street View."

"Stop being a smart-ass," Eddie growled. "Jess said it perfectly earlier: How did a merry-go-round get here, if there are no ways in or out and the tree line is a hundred years old? I mean, the place can't just be an island in the middle of a remote forest. Can it?"

"Why not? If this place was built for some fucked-up reason, they wouldn't exactly put it in plain view of a highway."

"I mean, how many people would it take to do that?"

"Does it fucking matter?" Greg shot back.

As annoying as the con man was, he had a fair point. Right now, the construction details of this town were irrelevant. Then again, so was pretty much everything that had come out of Greg's mouth.

Eddie peered between the trees for any depressions in snow wide enough to allow a vehicle to maze through.

No route out of the town appeared obvious.

The only way to discover a secret path was to enter the forest. Check areas where the trees had protected the ground from snowfall.

"We have to explore deeper," he said. "Check the—"

"Wait!" Trinity shrieked. "What the hell is that?"

Eddie spun to face her, startled by the sudden outburst. He followed Trinity's frantic stare into the forest. And rested his eyes on a sight that made him bolt rigid.

A splayed leg protruded from the side of a spruce tree. Blue jeans and a sneaker, caked in frost. The limb was still as a statue.

"Holy shit," Greg muttered.

Jess's and Eddie's eyes met. He motioned his head toward the leg, and they headed straight for the spruce.

His heart pounded. Not through fear about what they were about to see; that much was obvious by the absolute stillness, the state of the clothes, and the weather. But about the possible act of violence that had happened here recently.

Both slowed as they neared.

Jess rounded the trunk first. She looked down, gasped, and twisted away.

Eddie moved in front of her.

Bile instantly rose in his throat.

A man lay flat on his back. His plaid shirt and jeans had frozen solid, and his static hands were raised a few inches by his side, semi-clenched. The blood that had drenched the back of his head and the surrounding ground had transformed into a crimson, icy pool.

Eddie retched a few times, and cupped his hand around his mouth.

He'd seen a few brutal things in his time. A gang-related stabbing in a nightclub he used to frequent. Being the first on the scene at a head-on vehicle collision on the outskirts of Sackets Harbor. His uncle having a fatal heart attack at a Labor Day party. And his father . . .

But this . . .

A heavy chunk of log rested on top of the man's face. If he still had a face. The dense piece of wood must have been repeatedly hammered down, crushing his features, because it sat level with his ears.

Looking at the remains of the man, Eddie could not get a singular thought out of his mind: the pulp left behind when using an old-fashioned apple press to make cider.

He dry-heaved again.

There was something primal and bone-chilling about the attack. It stank of rage and insanity. The man had probably been dead well before the full extent of the damage had been inflicted. Repeated heavy blows to a lifeless corpse had to be the work of a psychopath.

And so was filling a wine bottle full of acid.

Jess moved to Eddie's shoulder. "You think he was kidnapped and brought here, like us?"

"I'm not sure. Looks like he's been here for a while."

"You think?"

Eddie had no real clue. His investigative and forensic skills only extended to what he had picked up on *CSI: Miami*. And even then, they always had the help of fancy equipment to back up their snappy dialogue.

However, he wanted to be nowhere near whoever carried out this act. His already healthy degree of paranoia had now rocketed into orbit. He needed to get away from this madness. His mind raced through the group's limited options.

They realistically had two. And both seemed dire.

It was stay in town or head out blindly into the wilderness, not knowing which direction to travel. It could be a hundred miles before they reached civilization or help.

"You think the old couple did this?" Jess asked.

"I don't see how," Eddie scoffed. He gazed between the trees at the seemingly undisturbed ground. "For starters, how did they get him here? Second, they wouldn't have had the strength to bash his face in with a log that size."

"Maybe the guy from the church did this?"

"Or maybe this *is* the guy from the church." He waved at Greg and Trinity to come over. "Look at this."

Trinity shook her head. "Are you for real?"

"Not a chance in hell," Greg called out.

"Then ignore the body. But we're going deeper into the forest. If we find nothing, we double back to the church for warmth and to regroup."

"Is that our best play?" Jess whispered before the other two arrived.

"Look, the last thing I wanna do is go back to town. But freezing to death in the woods sounds worse. Let's cross that bridge when we come to it. We press on into the forest a bit farther, and only turn back when we absolutely must."

Trinity and Greg slowly headed over to the large spruce,

though both avoided checking out the corpse. Everyone moved several yards deeper into the forest, then stopped to face each other in a small clearing.

"That's two dead," Greg said between shivering breaths. "Who knows how many more have been killed. So what's your grand plan, Eddie?"

"We pick a direction and head directly away from town. If we find nothing, we double back, warm up for a bit, and pick a new direction. And repeat."

"Got it. So the plan is to walk blindly until we eventually starve to death."

"Yeah, dick, that's the plan," Eddie said, scowling. "Don't push me. Or how about you take the lead, boss?"

The two men stared at each other, unflinching. The arrogant, middle-aged salesman had apparently been a predator in the past, but he was way out of his depth here. One more step toward Eddie, and Greg would find out the difference between duping senior citizens out of their pension and taking on a man with very little to lose.

"Let's go, Greg," Trinity hissed. "We can't fuck around."

Greg whispered something under his breath and turned to take point, leading the group deeper into the forest.

Trinity followed behind him as they cut a path close to trees, avoiding the snowiest parts of the ground; Jess went next, and Eddie took up the rear. For the first time, he considered ditching them. Greg and Trinity provided about as much protection as a bobble hat on the deck of the *Titanic*—post–iceberg strike.

"I think you made the right call," Jess whispered quietly to Eddie.

"Let's hope so. We're all flying blind here."

"Look at it this way. If we need to come up with another plan, I, for one, would rather make it miles from this town."

He nodded. "True enough. The problem is, we could be miles from anywhere."

She let out a resigned sigh, sending a cloud of misting breath into the forest.

Eddie looked over his shoulder at the distant buildings.

Every step farther away from that town made him feel better. But only slightly. He struggled to believe that whoever had put them here would just allow everyone to walk away.

For all he knew, the group was marching toward their own deaths.

12

ess stayed to the right of the group while they slowly cut a path between the trees. Overhead, drifting clouds had blocked out the sun's faint heat, and the forest had once again transformed to near darkness under the dense canopy of evergreens.

She snaked around trunks, stepping on the frozen, crunchy bed of pine needles that had dropped in the fall. Every few seconds, she glanced in all directions, mindful of the fact that the man who'd fled the church was probably in close proximity.

And mindful of the fact that she couldn't truly rely on any of the remaining survivors. Whether this situation would change remained highly questionable.

A crow's caw shattered the silence.

Jess froze next to an icy stream.

For a moment, she thought she'd seen a streak of blood in the water. But it was just a rotten twig, bobbing aimlessly downstream. The nonstop adrenaline rush of this situation was clearly affecting her.

She squeezed the wrench—her makeshift weapon—into a tighter grip. Strode over the stream. Her foot slipped on the opposite bank and she staggered forward a few paces.

Jess threw out an arm and grabbed the nearest trunk to stop herself from crashing onto the forest floor. The sharp bark ripped into her palm.

She grimaced as she looked down at the red marks.

None of the group seemed to notice as they headed toward a section of the forest with fewer trees. However, the searing pain and her surroundings had shot a vivid memory to the forefront of her mind. Her first taste of horror in the woods when she was only a teenager . . .

Sixteen years ago . . .

Jess at Nineteen

Jess crept through the forest at the back of the private estate. She held her skirt against the side of her legs to stop it from snagging on the undergrowth. She heard the distant sound of shouts from the house party, but she had purposely moved away.

She felt like a spare part at these events.

Jocks in heat, chugging and hollering. Freshman girls showing too much skin in the hopes of a free beer or to garner the attention of some guy. Everyone getting blind drunk while suffering eardrum damage from the incessant blast of repetitive music.

That aside, she knew it was part of the fabric when it came to college. And she had to take a role in the show. "The easiest way through life," her dad had once told her, "was to always be an insider. Play the game, regardless of your feelings, and a time will come when you'll be the one dictating proceedings."

Her father's words had sounded profound at the time, though on reflection as she moved through the woods, they seemed as hollow as the dead tree to her left.

The scent of marijuana carried on the breeze, coming from directly ahead. Pungent and skunk-like. She'd never liked it, despite always receiving a healthy amount of peer pressure to take a few drags.

Jess slowed her stride.

Pale moonlight shone through the trees, silhouetting a tall, muscular figure. He leaned slumped against a tree trunk. Took a long pull of a joint, its embers casting a glow on his face. Next, he started to scroll on his phone.

It was Kyle McHenry.

The biggest-ass clown at college. Loudmouthed and brash, with his father's money to burn. Always with slicked-back hair and wearing a tight polo shirt. But he was also potentially the most dangerous person to meet on a walk through a remote area of the property. In the past year, he had been accused of two sexual assaults. Rumors had spread of more. Almost everyone knew he was guilty, but when a building on campus is named after your family, it's easy to get away with most anything.

A twig snapped under Jess's shoe.

She sucked in a sharp breath. Went to duck behind a tree, but it was too late to find cover from his beady eyes.

Kyle's head had snapped in her direction.

"Who's there?" he demanded.

"Sorry," Jess spluttered. "I'll be on my way."

"Whoa, whoa, whoa, hold up a second."

She stood paralyzed, heart pounding, arms rigid by her sides.

Kyle took one more drag of his joint, held it in his lungs for a few moments, and exhaled a large cloud of smoke. He stood and headed toward Jess at a fast walk.

Her senses told her to back away, but before she could react he'd reached to within inches of Jess, towering over her, gazing down through bleary eyes with a fixed smile. There was no joy in his expression. It was cold, tense, and predatory. And he reeked of weed and booze.

"If I didn't know any better," he said, "I'd say you were spying on me."

Jess took a step back, but Kyle stayed close.

"I swear," she protested, "I wasn't."

"You just happened to stumble across me way out here? I call bullshit."

"Believe me, I had no idea you were here."

Kyle looked Jess up and down. The intensity of his gaze made her physically uncomfortable. It was almost as if his eyes had the uncanny ability to make the hairs on her neck prickle with revulsion. She began to sweat, despite the cool fall air.

"Wait, I've seen you around a few times," he said. "You help out at the library, don't you?"

"Yes."

"What's your name?"

Jess hesitated with a response. It felt like telling this jerk her name would somehow give him more power over her.

"I said what's your name?" he asked more forcefully.

"Jessica."

Kyle half-smiled. "See? Was that so hard? I'm just playing."

Something about the grin creeped her out. It was crooked, curling at one end, drooping at the other. Probably a result of inbreeding a few generations ago in his family tree.

"Well, Jessica the library assistant, it seems to me there are only three possible reasons you're out here right now. One, you're looking to take a hit." He motioned at the joint in his hand.

She shook her head no.

"Two," he said, "you're looking to bust me for smoking up in the woods."

"I swear, I wasn't."

"I see. So maybe it's the third reason."

He rested his hand on her shoulder and began to slide it down her arm, caressing the back of his fingers against her exposed flesh.

Kyle let out a satisfied groan. He reached for her chest.

Fight-or-flight mode kicked in.

Jess agonized over her next move. She knew she could react quicker than Kyle—he appeared high and drunk. At the moment, though, she was well within his reach. And despite being a douche, he was far stronger than her.

But Jess had no plans on becoming his next assault victim. The next name to hit the college rumor mill, with everyone giving her apologetic pitying looks.

Before he could touch her again, she thrust her shoe toward his shin.

Her shoe connected with a hard thud against bone.

He grunted as he stumbled back a few paces.

The joint dropped from his hand and disappeared into the underbrush.

Jess rushed around him and sprinted for a darker part of the forest. A place where it wouldn't be easy for him to locate her.

Within seconds, footsteps pounded the ground in hot pursuit.

"You bitch!" he shouted, as he gave chase.

Jess weaved between the trees, pulling away from the wheezing jerk. She scanned to her left and right, searching for a hiding place before she reached the perimeter fence.

Eventually, she spotted a huge boulder next to a large oak tree. A quick glance over the shoulder confirmed Kyle was too far away to see her.

Jess dove behind the boulder. She pressed her back against the cold stone. Tried to regulate her breathing so it wouldn't give away her hiding spot. This part of the property was even farther from the house than she'd been. Nobody would hear a scream, no matter how desperate the cries might be.

Kyle's clumsy footsteps thumped in her direction.

She patted the ground until her hand hit a rock. It weighed around five pounds. Good enough to inflict serious damage if required, though she hoped it wouldn't come to that.

Kyle stepped even closer to the boulder. She guessed he was only yards away.

Then he stopped.

The forest fell silent.

Jess swallowed hard. She guessed he was listening, looking for any signs of movement, any clues on the ground for her direction of travel.

Eventually, he said, "Why don't you come out here, Jessica the librarian. Maybe we got off on the wrong foot."

She shuddered at the smug tone of his voice. He was enjoying this.

Silence returned once more for a painful minute or so. Jess knew it was wishful thinking that Kyle would get bored and leave. His ego wouldn't let him give her a pass. To him, she guessed, this hunt only had one natural conclusion.

"I know you're out here," Kyle announced. "How about this: I'll allow you to make it up to me. I have a few ideas."

His footsteps moved closer to the boulder.

Jess was in a crouching position, preparing to move fast if he came within a few feet. The adrenaline pumping through her veins made her entire body quiver and her heart practically explode out of her chest.

Kyle's hand reached over and grabbed the shoulder of her dress.

She sprung up and attempted to back away.

He grabbed a fistful of her clothing and held her tight, peering into her eyes with a snarling smile. "Where do you think you're—"

Jess smashed the rock against the side of his head. For a brief, terrifying moment, he stared at her, expressionless. Then, thankfully, Kyle collapsed backward into a group of ferns.

Moonlight reflected off the blood that trickled down the side of his face and neck. His eyes were half-open as he groaned, woozy. But she knew the force of the blow meant he wasn't getting back up anytime soon.

"Leave me the hell alone!" Jess screamed.

Kyle mumbled something unintelligible, still dazed from the blunt force. Hesitantly, Jess approached closer and stood over him. Her fear had quickly dissipated, replaced with a feeling of exhilaration.

"I think it's fair to say," she said, while looking down pitifully at the bleeding man, "you had this coming. Wouldn't you agree?"

Present Day

"Jess. Jess," Eddie said, shaking her arm.

She instantly broke out of her trance.

"What's up? It seemed like you were on another planet."

"It's nothing," she responded. "Just an old memory. Sorry. Let's keep moving."

Frost had formed on Eddie's eyebrows and stubble, but determination burned in his eyes. He grabbed her arm and encouraged her away from the pine tree.

Soon, they were catching up to the other members of the

group. Greg and Trinity had made it to a clearer part of the forest and had paused to wait. Both looked thoroughly ticked off.

Once again, she considered Eddie as easily more likable and a lot more proactive than the other two. And he was definitely a million times more likable than that jerk Kyle McHenry from years ago. But deep down, Jess knew that for him to be here, trapped along with her, Eddie was harboring dark secrets of his own.

And those secrets were bound to surface, sooner or later.

13

Eddie stumbled through an exposed section of prickly underbrush, his breath ragged and harsh. Behind him, Jess followed with more assured movements. She'd snapped out of her haze pretty fast. He wondered if—like him—she had been contemplating her own secrets. After all, considering Greg's and Tank's histories, and Eddie's capture while trying to rob the old couple, it was now blindingly obvious that everyone had some dark reasons for being here.

My real reason, though . . .

Is it just a simple trap?

Did the old couple lurk around the store, waiting for strangers to enter, then follow them in and tempt crime by flashing cash? Seeing which sucker would fall into their demented trap? It seemed unlikely, as the store workers would have been in on it too.

The idea was too elaborate, but with this town as context . . .

Maybe. Maybe not.

Would anyone really do this to a low-grade thief? Even despite what he had done . . .

A more disturbing notion shot to the front of his mind. Eddie could have been a long-term target for an unknown enemy. Which meant somebody had been watching him. Stalking. Waiting. Setting traps until the perfect opportunity had presented itself in the Old Forge store.

But why?

Granted, his life had hardly been littered with glory. The longest he'd held down a job was six months at a Chick-fil-A. As for his other "jobs," there were a few burglaries, some car thefts, a couple of years selling knockoff goods on Canal Street. To him, though, none of his crimes had warranted this brutal judgment. Neither did stealing a purse. His conclusion was that he must have inadvertently pissed off the wrong person—at the wrong time. Given the amount of people he'd fucked over in life, the list of potential suspects was practically endless.

And as for his worst offense, no one in the world knew about that . . .

Right?

Eddie rounded a couple of firs and approached Greg. The salesman wore a perpetual, negative grimace, and he had a very punchable face. The kind of guy you'd like to see accidentally fall off a cliff while taking a selfie in a YouTube video.

Trinity rolled her eyes like Eddie had slowed the whole group down.

Why, exactly, is she here?

The howling wind that blew between the trees seemed to carry an eerie whisper, as if the forest itself held secrets he also wasn't meant to know. He cast a quick glance behind him to make sure Jess had kept up with his brisk pace.

"Don't worry about me," she said. "Everyone keep moving."

He nodded. Turned to the other two. "You guys okay?"

"Yeah, yeah, I'm fine," Greg muttered through clenched teeth. "Just twisted my ankle, I think."

"How did you do that?"

"How you think? I rolled it."

"Can you keep going?"

"Like I've got a choice?"

Eddie knew better than to ask any more questions. Greg had proven to be negative, verbose, and short-fused during their limited time together. A bad recipe for their current plight.

The four of them had to make progress, and there was no time to slow down for minor injuries or petty squabbles. Not when the feeling of being watched seemed to grow stronger with each passing moment.

Eddie took the lead again to dictate a faster pace. He surged through the clearing and reentered the gloom of the forest. With the sun gone, the mercury had plunged again. His bones ached from the cold, and his stomach rumbled from lack of food. Fear drove him toward another clearing, though. Several yards from it, he stopped, momentarily frozen by the sight ahead.

A shaft of daylight beamed through the canopy, brightening a small, nondescript concrete building. Square with gray walls, a tiled roof, and a steel door with an external bolt across it, locked in place with a heavy-duty padlock.

He fixed his gaze on the roof.

A modern satellite dish and a whip antenna aimed skyward.

The sight of modern technology made Eddie edge back a few steps.

The building had brought a momentary sense of relief, but that had quickly transformed into a cause for concern. The satellite dish saw to that.

Is it shelter or something more sinister?

Everyone took cover behind a group of firs and silently observed the structure.

Tree stumps and a knee-high blanket of brown ferns surrounded the building. No tire tracks were visible on the sheltered parts of the ground.

"I don't see any footpath leading to the door," Jess finally said.

"Don't mean shit," Trinity shot back. "Those security cameras in town were transmitting somewhere. Looks like we've found the place."

"She's right," Greg said. "I mean, why else was it built away from town?"

Eddie shook his head. "Don't know."

"If nobody is home," Trinity said, "we might have found a way to contact civilization."

"Sure. Like they'd just allow us to walk in and radio the cops," Eddie replied.

"I'll go, Trinity," Greg said. "We can't let these two slow us down any longer."

Eddie gave him a look of disbelief. "Slow you down?"

"That's right. Now back off."

Greg held the steel pipe over his shoulder and strode forward.

"Wait," Jess hissed. "We need to think about this first."

"Think about what?" Greg gave a dismissive shake of the head. "I've been slashed with a knife, I'm starving, I've got borderline hypothermia. That satellite dish might be our ticket out of here."

"But what if someone is inside?"

He tapped the pipe against his palm. "Then they'll wish they weren't."

"Just wait," Eddie pleaded. "Let's watch for a few minutes, not make any rash moves."

Greg spun away without replying and set off toward the building. It seemed with a hint of salvation in sight, he had finally grown some courage. He broke through the ferns and waded with purpose toward the front door.

Eddie scanned every direction for signs of danger. Greg's theory and course of action seemed like wishful thinking. The only guarantee in Eddie's mind was that this building would not be a straightforward ticket to safety, just like everything else they had encountered since waking.

Trinity went to follow Greg, but Jess grabbed her by the shoulder.

"Get your hand off me, girl," Trinity said.

"You don't know—"

A metallic crack echoed through the forest.

A chain rattled.

Then a bloodcurdling, long scream pierced the air.

Greg collapsed out of view.

Eddie rushed forward, crashing through the ferns until he realized that something in the undergrowth could take him down. He staggered to a slow pace, peering between the brown leaves until he reached Greg's side.

Blood had already started to surround Greg's injured left leg. A large, hidden bear trap had snapped around his calf. The razor-sharp teeth had bitten through his trousers into the flesh of his calf and shin. Possibly an inch deep, piercing through to the bone. The trap itself was chained firmly into a concrete base.

"Holy shit," Eddie mumbled.

Greg roared in agony. He tried to sit up and force the trap open, but flopped back down, writhing. The veins in his neck and temple throbbed. He gasped out an agonized scream.

Eddie dropped to his knees. He grabbed the metal jaws, attempting to heave them open. They didn't budge, despite him giving it everything.

"Get the fucking thing off of me," Greg begged. "Please!"

"It's no use," Eddie said, gasping. "It won't move."

Trinity and Jess headed over. They stared down with wild-eyed expressions.

"Gimme a hand!" Eddie ordered, desperate to pry the device loose.

Jess helped him pull on the metal, but it remained rigidly in place. Which came as no surprise. The trap had been designed to not open once it had been sprung and ensnared a predator.

Eddie and Jess wedged a stick between the trap's jaws and tried to pry it apart. It worked for a moment and opened the teeth a couple of millimeters.

Greg screamed out in newfound agony.

"FUCKING STOP!"

The group immediately released the stick, and the trap slammed shut once again, ripping deeper into his flesh.

"What?!" Eddie said. "Why'd you stop us?!"

"Guys, take a look," Jess said, pointing down.

Eddie leaned in close to examine the trap. Whoever had planted it had sharpened its teeth into serrated edges, post-purchase. Meaning that pulling it apart would tear the flesh from the victim's bones on its way out.

"What the fuck . . ."

Greg screamed again, long and loud. Blood poured from his wounds. His face grew a paler shade of white and it looked like he was going into shock.

But his being caught in a trap had other implications as well. If nobody knew the group had made it to this part of the forest, they did now. Eddie's mind raced as he assessed the situation. If they couldn't pry the device apart for risk of tearing Greg apart, they needed to at least break the chain and cut the trap loose from the concrete pad.

The hardware store back in town.

It was a long shot, but there was no other way.

"We have to go back to town," Eddie said.

"You can't be serious," Trinity shot back. "For what?"

"The hardware store might have something we can use to cut Greg free. And get this door open. It's our only choice."

"I'm with Eddie," Jess said. "We can't just leave him here to die."

Trinity glared toward the town. "The only thing waiting back there is more death."

"You see any other option?" Eddie asked. "If we don't break that chain, Greg either bleeds . . . *or freezes* . . . to death. The clock's ticking."

"For fuck's sake," Greg cried out through the pain, straining to get his words out. "Just get your asses moving, and please hurry back."

Eddie knelt over him. "We'll be back as soon as we can, I promise."

Trinity, Jess, and Eddie left Greg sprawled between the ferns. It took a minute of walking before the sounds of his suffering vanished in the wind.

Sure, it was dangerous leaving him on his own, but it was no bigger a risk than returning to a place with two deaths already confirmed. At a moment's notice, any of them could encounter a maniac who was hell-bent on killing every one of them in some sickening, elaborate way.

This thought spurred Eddie on.

He broke into a slow jog.

The forest seemed even darker and more foreboding as they retraced their steps to the outskirts of town. And soon, the mutilated, frozen corpse loomed back into view. The sense of being watched by a motivated psychopath increased to a suffocating weight on Eddie's shoulders.

Trinity and Jess flanked him as they neared the start of the cobblestone road. A gust of wind whipped through the main street, welcoming them back with a blast of ice-cold air. The town looked lifeless, with its fluttering awnings and creaking timber frames, though Eddie knew better than to judge on appearances.

"Let's do this fast," he said. "Straight to the store and back to Greg. The sooner we free him, the quicker we get the hell away from here."

Neither Jess nor Trinity replied as they hit the street.

The grim expressions of the two women told him that they likely held thoughts similar to what he was truly thinking. The chances of breaking the chain holding the bear trap were slim at best. And if they did find something in the hardware store for the job, Greg's injury would make him a serious liability in their quest for survival.

But the alternative was leaving Greg behind.

Eddie was guilty of a lot of things, and one of his crimes had undoubtedly led him here, but leaving a man to suffer a miserable death was not part of his makeup.

Not anymore, at least.

14

ow clouds had gathered over the reproduced town of Old
Forge, adding to the overwhelming claustrophobia. Eddie,
Jess, and Trinity moved in a tight group, their footsteps
crunching over the snow-covered street.

Eddie visually searched through every window and doorway
of the nearest buildings. And every alleyway leading to the forest. At any moment, he expected a dark figure to burst out of a
well-chosen hiding place to end their lives.

But Eddie wouldn't make that an easy job.

He held his weapon in his frostbitten hand, knowing his grip
had grown weaker from the temperature and lack of food and
that his body was nowhere near full strength. Despite all of this,
he was ready for the battle ahead.

Eddie wanted to meet those responsible for this collective trap.

His desperation and sense of doom had slowly begun to
morph into anger. The group was now effectively a wounded
animal in a corner, especially Greg, whose distant, unrelenting
wail carried through the forest pitifully.

The audible anguish was a stark contrast to the bright and
cheerful Christmas decorations adorning the buildings' windows.

It all still felt unbelievable.

The hardware store lay halfway along the main street, sand-
wiched between the diner and bakery. An easily observable
location for any prying eye.

Eddie headed over at a fast walk, peering at the street's second-story windows. Each one provided a great vantage point to watch the group's return.

For a split second, he thought he spotted movement behind an upper window of the inn. But on second inspection it was a drape, twitching back and forth, likely from an internal draft.

He had no shreds of shame at overreacting to any signs of movement.

Better to stay frosty . . .

He laughed to himself at the thought. With temperatures below zero, he had no choice *but* to stay frosty. Eddie intuitively understood that the minute he switched off would probably be his last.

"You really think we'll find anything of use?" Trinity whispered.

"Well, we found medical supplies in the pharmacy, right?" said Jess.

"True. But this place creeps me the fuck out."

"Ditto."

"Let's just take it nice and slow," Jess said.

Eddie nodded, trying to hide the unease that gnawed in his stomach. There had to be something of use in this snapshot of a bygone era. The town hall had appeared to be in mid-construction, and somebody had to maintain the other buildings to stop them from rotting and falling to the ground. The crisp paintwork on the signage, the pristine never-been-used merry-go-round, and the tidiness of the church suggested that much.

As the group reached the hardware store, the sign above the entrance swayed in the faint breeze, its rusty chain giving off an ominous clink.

Eddie crept underneath the awning and stopped a few paces from the door. It had a clear glass panel with a retro, stenciled gold logo across the pane and the name *Old Forge Hardware* etched in the wood paneling. Daylight streamed through, allowing him to see parts of the shadowy interior.

A jumble of faded cardboard boxes sat on top of a wooden counter. Shelves lined the walls, containing numerous dark objects. And at the back, larger items had been neatly piled against the wall.

He turned to the other two. "It isn't empty, that's for sure."

"Go for it," Trinity said.

Eddie paused to take a deep breath. His trepidation over entering another building held him back for a moment, unsure about the possible dangers ahead.

He thrust the handle down and shoved.

Locked.

Eddie retreated a step, raised his boot, and rammed it against the spot where he thought the lock might be.

The door boomed inward, giving much more easily than he'd expected, and smashed against a stopper.

Eddie winced at the sound it had created.

A layer of dust dropped from the frame, creating a thin cloud in the entrance.

Then something clicked above the door, like a latch or . . .

Eddie's eyes widened. The glinting head of an axe swung down and out in a pendulum motion, slicing through the dust and whistling directly toward his face. Terror rooted him to the spot. Every instinct pleaded with him to move, but Eddie's body refused to obey.

This is it . . .

In the blink of an eye, Jess hammered into his side.

They both flew to the left, and his shoulder battered against the store's timber deck. Eddie immediately scrambled to a crouch, heart racing, and looked back at the entrance. He sucked in a deep breath, staring in horrified astonishment as the axe swung back inside. A second later, it powered back out, and stopped rigid with a dull thud as it leveled with the doorway.

Trinity spun to bolt for the forest, but turned back almost immediately.

Jess climbed to her feet and extended a hand down.

"Holy fuck," Eddie exclaimed, grabbing Jess's hand and pulling himself up. "You saved my life."

"I wouldn't say that too soon. I think we've still got a long way to go."

He gave her a faint smile. "Thanks anyway. I owe you one."

They both moved over to inspect the booby trap.

The axe's head was forged out of solid metal with a seven-inch blade, sharp enough to break skin with the lightest of touches. Eddie craned his head inside the doorway. The long handle had been attached to a wheeled mechanism.

He shuddered as he recalled the slight delay from the door's opening to the initial swing. The trap had probably been designed and primed to hold for a few seconds. Enough time for an unsuspecting person to step forward before the axe buried itself into their chest.

"It's pretty basic," Jess said.

"Pretty damned deadly if you ask me," Trinity said from behind.

"Think about it," Eddie said. "The acid in the wine bottle. The bear trap. This axe. It's clear someone wants us dead, but maybe they don't have the guts to do it themselves."

"They had the guts to bash some dude's face in," Trinity said.

"Perhaps," Jess added. "Or it was done after he was already dead."

Trinity slowly shook her head, muttering under her breath.

However, Jess's logic had sounded reasonable to Eddie, though he couldn't process the implications. His mind was still scrambled from his most recent near-death experience. But he told himself to get a grip. Move ahead with their plan instead of having a meltdown.

"I'm heading inside," he said. "Jess, gimme a hand. Trinity, keep a lookout."

Eddie entered the store and gazed through the dim light.

No red lights on the ceiling or the walls.

No cameras studying their every move.

The floorboards creaked beneath his boots. He looked down for trip wires or any other traps he could spot. He extended a hand in front of himself and wafted it, checking to see if a length of piano wire had been strung across the room. Eventually, he circled behind the counter and searched the shelves. To his surprise, he found boxes of nuts and bolts, small screwdrivers and wrenches, six-inch nails, and plastic cable ties. He stuffed a few items in his pockets, thinking they might come in handy later.

But he found nothing that could help break the chains holding Greg to the ground.

Jess yanked a filthy blanket from a square pile, revealing a stack of thick wooden railroad ties. Next, she rifled through a few of the moldy boxes near the back of the room, throwing their contents over her shoulder as she looked for something useful.

Eddie moved to the opposite side of the store. He slid open the drawers of a huge antique cabinet.

A host of dark metal objects sat in the second one.

Then, among the disarray, he spotted a pair of bolt cutters.

"Bingo," he said with no joy in his voice.

Eddie closed his hands around the cold, reassuring grip of the metal handles. He lifted the tool out, then snipped the blades together a few times to test the functionality.

"You think that'll work?" Jess asked.

"Can't imagine finding anything better."

She gave him a firm nod. "Then let's get back to Greg."

They exited the store, back into the freezing, windswept street. Trinity had dutifully remained under the awning, arms wrapped around herself for warmth.

Eddie flashed her the bolt cutters and she immediately turned for the forest. All three headed back in Greg's direction with the utmost caution.

This had been a successful mission. However, the "success" was only a minor climb against the deadly mountain they faced.

And Greg still needed freeing.

That is, *if* he hadn't already bled out.

15

The throbbing pain in Greg's leg had the intensity of an erupting super-volcano. Bile rocketed up his throat. His entire body shook and shivered. He lay helpless on his back as a biting chill penetrated his jacket.

He let out a few ragged breaths. He knew the group had only been away for twenty minutes, but to him it felt like an eternity.

Although he was exhausted, he didn't dare close his eyes. Not even for a moment. He remembered reading somewhere that hypothermia victims fell asleep when they were close to death. So instead, he looked between the trees for any signs of the group's return. Forced his eyes open. Focused on the pain.

His fate was literally in the hands of three unskilled strangers.

He hated that.

But he had no other choice at the moment.

It infuriated him that his courage had led to this injury. The other three had just sat back and let him take all the risks. They owed him. Big time.

The icy grip of winter which had invaded the forest seemed to close around him tighter by the second. Each of his trembling breaths produced larger freezing clouds, potentially giving away his presence. He reached down to the trap and grabbed the jaws. He weakly tried to free himself, though he knew deep down that he lacked the physical strength, or the will.

An excruciating bolt of pain shot up his leg. He pursed his lips tightly, attempting to stay silent through the agony.

He knew this trap would have killed anyone else in the group by now, but he was different. Greg was a born fighter. A born winner. His grandfather had taught him that from the start.

He wheezed into a sitting position, tears streaming down his face.

He shook his head in utter madness, astounded by the plan some sadistic asshole had executed against a few *relatively* innocent people . . .

It had to have been one of his former clients who had forced him into this fate. He had no doubt in his mind. A bitter pensioner with nothing better to do than exact revenge on a man who had made a few wrong investments.

Sure, Greg himself always came out financially on top, while making sure to live modestly so as to not attract too much attention. He had the self-awareness to realize that those who had lost their savings had no desire to see him driving around in his Cybertruck. He saved that vehicle for his countryside house.

Yes, a bitter, bitter pensioner. Some old fuck.

The fact was, he had never lost other people's money on purpose. But shit happens. Besides, most of those old fools had plenty in the bank. Big fat nest eggs for their entitled children and spoiled grandkids, who would squander it within a year of their deaths.

If some pissed-off former client was to blame for this mess, did Greg's actions warrant this kind of response? Not for a second. He swore that if he survived this ordeal, he would have his revenge.

He would bring down hell on whoever had put him through this.

They would regret the day they messed with Greg—

A rustling in the woods shook him from his building fury.

A moment later, the forest returned to near silence once again.

Probably nothing.

Though in this town, he couldn't rule anything out.

Greg quieted his breathing. Listened for any sound above the moaning wind.

He heard the gentle rustle again. Distant at first, just a faint whisper in the trees, but it drew nearer with each passing second. His mind raced, trying to make sense of the bizarre stutter-stop approach.

Why would the group be sneaking back toward me?

Had they been chased, and were being overly cautious?

No . . . it must be someone else.

The rustling grew even louder, punctuated by grunts, deep breaths, and heavy stomps. Greg twisted and turned desperately to see who was approaching. But the merciless trap, crushing his leg with an even force, wouldn't allow him to see in which direction the sound was coming from.

The mental image of the log resting on that man's crushed face raced to the front of his mind.

All he could do was listen, helpless and vulnerable, with his back toward the approaching hunter carrying a new section of log with Greg's name on it.

But why is he approaching so strangely?

An image formed in his mind. A tall, local hillbilly in a plaid shirt. Scarred face, hands as big as shovels, IQ in the negative digits, carrying an oversized sledgehammer that was destined to connect with Greg's skull.

He imagined other twisted possibilities, each one more

horrifying than the last. The hillbilly skinning him alive, then casually sprinkling salt over his writhing body. A group of cannibals feasting on him and filming the entire thing for their entertainment. Didn't he see a doc like that once?

His imagination . . . and fear . . . ran wild with the possibilities.

But the reality was far worse.

A nightmare beyond his wildest imagination finally appeared in his peripheral vision, snapping him back from his bleak thoughts.

A hulking silhouette emerged from the shadows, lumbering closer with each ponderous step. It was a bear, moving toward him with a slow, deliberate curiosity. It had a dished face, rounded ears, and a shoulder hump.

A goddamned grizzly!

But in Upstate New York? How?

Greg held in a scream.

It was useless to try to defend himself. Any sign of aggression, and the grizzly would tear him to shreds like a rag doll.

His only option was to play dead.

The bear moved to within a few feet behind him, close enough that Greg could twist his head and now see it clearly.

The grizzly had matted and stained fur, a testament to the harsh life it had led in this unforgiving wilderness. It was also massive. Easily six or seven hundred pounds. The bear's dark eyes fixed on Greg, and for a moment their gazes locked in a silent, primal exchange.

Time seemed to stand still as the bear drew to within a couple of feet of Greg, its hot breath fogging around its mouth and nostrils.

Greg tensed, heart hammering. He knew that any sudden

movement could provoke the beast, sealing his fate. He lay as still as possible, praying that the bear's curiosity would wane and it would simply move on.

The grizzly tilted its head as it sniffed the air. It was as if the creature sensed that something was amiss, something was out of the ordinary. Greg struggled to remain motionless. His life depended on the bear's next move.

Then, to his relief, the grizzly grunted softly, as if satisfied with its inspection. It took a step back, its gaze never leaving him.

The beast eventually turned away, its enormous form disappearing back into the woods. Greg let out a deep sigh, his heart still pounding, the pain in his leg throbbing in time with the rhythm of his pulse. He was still trapped, still alone, but for now, at least, he was safe from the predator.

With renewed determination, Greg knew he had to hang on. He couldn't give in to fear or despair. The group would return, and together, they would free him. Until then, he would endure the freezing cold and the agonizing pain, drawing strength from the fleeting encounter with the grizzly bear that had, for reasons unknown, spared his life.

A moment later, the rustling sound returned, but this time with frantic, pounding footsteps.

Greg twisted his neck and peered through the trees.

His eyes widened.

The massive grizzly charged directly at him.

It crashed a paw down on his gut, and its razor-sharp claws tore through Greg's flesh and organs like they were papier-mâché.

His garbled scream echoed through the forest, crying out for help that would never arrive.

16

The cold gnawed at Jess's skin as she jogged through the frozen forest. Each step felt like lifting lead weights, and the icy wind clawed at her face. Eddie and Trinity followed closely behind. Both moving slower, grimacing with each step, but probably driven on by forlorn hope.

Jess had no such hope. Her decision process remained clinical. That was her only chance of seeing this through.

She cast her mind back to the deserted town. The empty buildings and eerie silence were enough to send shivers down anyone's spine. Added to that, the man who had fled the church was still on the loose, yet to reappear. He posed no direct threat . . . yet. And the group had a singular purpose.

There was no turning back for anyone.

Jess charged over the frozen pine needles, determined to make progress. This part of the forest seemed endless, with towering trees covered in heavy blankets of snow that threatened to drop at any moment.

They had to move faster. Greg was out there, stranded and cold, and possibly close to death. Jess's greatest desire was for him to still be alive when the group arrived back at the concrete bunker.

She picked up her pace again, nearing a sprint. Didn't care if the others couldn't keep up. Couldn't care less if they had a different priority from hers of finding Greg alive.

As she neared the location of the trap, she heard no cries of desperation.

Please don't be dead.

A moment after this thought, a guttural growl made her skid to a halt. Eddie and Trinity stopped close behind. All exchanged nervous glances.

"What the hell?" Trinity whispered.

"Sounds like an animal," Eddie replied.

"Keep moving," Jess ordered. "We can't afford to wait."

"Hold up." Trinity sucked in a couple of deep breaths. "Are you serious?"

Jess ignored the question. She advanced without caution, stepping from tree to tree, searching for any signs of life. Within thirty yards of the trap, the source of the growl came into view, stopping her dead in her tracks.

A huge grizzly bear stood over Greg. It sank its crimson-stained teeth into his stomach and ripped away chunks of flesh.

His body remained motionless as he was devoured.

"No," Jess breathed. "No, no, no."

Eddie rushed ahead.

He waved his bolt cutters and bellowed.

The grizzly gazed in the direction of the group. It let out a chilling growl that sounded through the forest. For a heartbeat, its eyes locked with Jess, as if sizing her up, like it was deciding whether she posed a threat to its meal.

"Help me scare it off!" Eddie said frantically. "It won't attack a group."

Jess pulled Trinity forward. They joined in yelling, waving weapons. The bear turned toward the group and roared back. It took a couple of steps away from Greg, its nose glistening with blood, readying itself to charge.

As Jess prepared herself mentally to run, something caught her eye.

On the verge of death, the partially consumed Greg limply raised his hand for a fleeting moment.

He's still alive!

Jess quickly eyed the ground. She found a cluster of frozen pine cones. Picked them up and launched them full force at the grizzly in rapid succession.

One of the cones connected directly, battering the bear's right eye.

The beast stood still for a moment, seemingly startled by the unexpected impact and the newfound aggression of its prey.

Jess held her breath for a moment, holding her ground, praying for the outcome she so desperately wanted.

Seemingly determining the fight was no longer worth the meal, the grizzly turned away from the group and lumbered back into the dense trees, eventually disappearing into a distant part of the forest.

"Let's give it a minute to be certain it's gone," Eddie whispered.

But Jess could no longer wait. Ignoring Eddie, she rushed over to Greg, dropping to her knees beside his mutilated body. His jacket and shirt had been ripped open. Claw marks scarred his upper chest, and his intestines were exposed and shredded.

The stench of partially digested food made her retch.

She reached down with a trembling hand and caressed his cheek.

Greg's lips parted to let out a shallow breath. His eyelids flickered open, and he focused on her.

Jess grabbed his hand.

He tried to say something, but he only managed a bloody gurgle.

"It's okay, Greg," she said. "Don't try to speak. I'm here. You're not alone."

She attempted an optimistic look to conceal her true emotions.

Seconds later, Greg's eyes glazed over, and he exhaled for the last time.

Jess shuddered.

She let go of his hand and bowed her head.

The others ran over, their faces etched with horror. Trinity covered her mouth, nearly vomiting at the gruesome sight, and quickly turned away.

Eddie stared at the scene, transfixed by the sheer brutality of the attack.

"My God . . ." he whispered, aghast.

The group stood there in silence for several minutes. Just like after Tank's death in the church, it appeared that the next words would be carefully chosen, and nobody seemed to possess them yet.

Finally, Eddie, who stared toward the distant part of the forest, asked, "I'm not crazy—that was a grizzly bear, right?"

"Yes," Jess said. "One hundred percent."

Eddie looked up for a second in thought. "You see the problem here?"

Both women stared at him without replying.

"There are no grizzlies in Upstate New York," he said.

Jess slowly nodded, understanding his implication.

"So," Eddie continued. "*Where the hell are we?*"

17

E ddie looked at the women without expectation in his eyes. His question had been rhetorical in nature. Truly, none of them had any clue where they were. And the longer this nightmare went on, the more the mystery deepened.

A grizzly, though?

It confused the hell out of him. His best guess was he had been taken to Montana . . . Idaho . . . Wyoming perhaps . . . Certainly not the Northeast.

Just how long were we knocked out?

"So," Jess asked. "What do we do now?"

"I say we check out what's inside that building," Eddie replied.

"You're not serious?" Trinity asked. "Greg was just killed trying to enter there."

"And you were nearly killed going into the hardware store," Jess added.

"Trust me, I remember." Eddie shrugged. "But what other choice do we have? There's a satellite dish on the roof, right? Maybe there's a phone or computer inside. Either way, we gotta find out, whether we like it or not."

Jess nodded. "All right. Then let's find out."

Trinity extended a flat palm toward the building. "You first, chief."

Eddie found her increasingly tiresome. He shot her a rapid glare as he brushed through the ferns toward the small, bunker-like concrete structure. He checked the ground before planting his boot, half-expecting another trap to rip his leg apart at any moment.

He couldn't get the bear out of his mind, though. Eddie gripped the bolt cutters tight, ready to swing at anyone . . . He listened for any signs of approaching wildlife, or the true enemy who had cast him in this horror show.

Jess kept close. Her presence continued to give him a breadcrumb of reassurance. Her gut instincts and outdoors skills gave him hope for their survival. She'd also saved his life when he froze.

But as for Trinity . . . her constant moaning served as a backdrop to their grim reality.

The reality was, everyone had to risk their lives trying to escape the grip of an unknown assassin, or they would freeze to death. One way or another, the clock was ticking.

As Eddie closed in on the metal entrance to the building, he had disturbing visions from the hardware store. The axe whooshing out of the dark doorway, nearly slicing him in half vertically.

He paused, and looked over his shoulder. Behind Trinity, he could still make out Greg's prone figure. His corpse lay flat on its back, mouth open like he was in mid-yawn, clothing shredded around his guts, and faint wisps of steam rising from his still-warm innards.

We're surrounded by death . . .

But only we can change that.

"There's a padlock and chain on the door," Eddie said.

"Could be another trap," Jess replied.

"True. Don't worry, though. I won't make the same mistake twice."

He headed to the side of the building, and used his elbow

to wipe frost from a small window, revealing opaque glass that wouldn't allow him to see inside.

Eddie moved back to the entrance and placed the cutter blades on the lock's shackle. He gave it a firm squeeze, and the metal snapped. He grabbed the steel door handle.

Jess offered him an approving nod.

He creaked the door outward, staying behind it for protection.

To his relief, no axe or person burst out. The interior room was quiet.

"It's clear," Jess said, peering inward. "Doesn't look like much inside."

Eddie stepped into the doorway to see for himself.

Pale light radiated through the small window in the eight-by-eight structure. A few cables hung from the ceiling over a dusty wooden table. There were no signs of any booby traps in the sparse interior. It looked like it hadn't been used in years . . . apart from the dozens of fresh newspaper clippings that had been purposefully glued to the wall behind the table.

That's odd.

Eddie advanced for a closer look.

The first clipping read, *"Boy, 9, Killed by Hit-and-Run Driver."* Another read, *"Manhunt for Hit-and-Run Driver, Still at Large."*

Eddie kept scanning the headlines: *"Funeral Service for Hit-and-Run Victim Planned for Thursday"* and *"Tragedy Remains Unsolved,"* detailing how a vehicle had swerved off Maguire Road and collided with a child on a skateboard, killing him instantly.

"What the hell is all this?" Eddie whispered to himself. He continued to scan the headlines.

Another one read, *"Police Recover Security Footage of Crash that Killed 9-Year-Old Boy."* Farther down, another clipping read *"Police Identify Car from Fatal Hit-and-Run."*

Eddie leaned in closer to the wall to read a newspaper clipping that had been circled in red marker. His eyes widened as he read the headline . . .

"Driver Arrested in Fatal Hit-and-Run Identified as Trinity Jackson."

"What the *hell* . . ." he mumbled, confused.

Eddie quickly scanned the article for key information. Security footage had captured Trinity's Jeep racing away from the scene of the hit-and-run with damage on the right side of the bumper. She'd attended a birthday party earlier that day at a local bar. Several witnesses had claimed they'd seen her drinking multiple shots of Jameson at the party, and was in no fit state to drive.

The headline on the final clipping said, *"Local Outrage as Killer Goes Free on Procedural Technicality."*

Eddie's mouth dropped open as the information sank in. He gazed back outside.

"Well?" Trinity asked.

"You . . . you'd better come take a look."

"I'm not going in there. Just tell me what it is."

"All these newspaper headlines are about . . ." Eddie paused, unsure how to say what he was about to say. "You."

"Huh?"

"It's about a hit-and-run. You killing someone with your car and going free."

Trinity bolted rigid. Her eyes darted between Eddie and Jess. "Is this some kind of sick joke?"

Eddie pointed at the clippings. "Come see for yourself."

Trinity's face turned beet red with anger. She sprinted over to the wall and began to tear the headlines down without even reading them, hand over hand. This action confirmed her guilt in Eddie's mind.

"Anything you wanna share with us, Trinity?" he asked.

"Yeah, this is all bullshit! It's some twisted joke."

"They look pretty real to me," Jess said.

"Fuck you, Jess. This entire town is some kind of sadistic mindfuck."

"Maybe this is why you're here, Trinity," Jess said. She walked inside and studied the clippings. "I mean, this is bad."

"I didn't fucking do anything, I swear!" she protested.

Eddie groaned. "Does it fucking matter?"

"Yeah, it does to me! I didn't kill a child!"

Jess turned toward her. "How did you know it was a child? I don't think Eddie mentioned that."

This response, finally, stopped Trinity's smart-assed comments. Instead, she crumpled the newspaper clippings and threw them onto the floor with trembling hands. Then, she bolted back outside.

Trinity's crime and reason for being here seemed clear enough, though it was way worse than Eddie's trying to pickpocket an elderly couple. But he had already guessed that everyone was guilty of something. The moral scale seemed irrelevant.

He headed outside after Trinity. "All right, let's keep going," he said. "There's nothing here."

"Nothing?" Trinity barked. "Some crazy psycho put false info about me here. They did it to stir up trouble. Don't you see that?"

Jess let out a long sigh. "Sounds like you're protesting too much."

"Me? Bitch, you probably did something way worse—"

"Stop!" Eddie shouted. "This solves jack shit. We keep moving away from the town. Find any form of civilization, transport, whatever, and get safe before we tear each other apart. We're all guilty of something, okay? It doesn't fucking matter or help us survive."

His booming voice appeared to have the desired impact.

Trinity gave him a tentative nod.

Jess led the group, and they headed away from the concrete building. She forged a path between the trees at a good pace. Eddie brought up the rear, giving encouragement to Trinity as she stumbled forward.

But he'd honestly had enough of her.

Enough of the lack of focus and derisive comments.

If it came to another life-and-death situation, and Trinity's attitude compromised the group—meaning his own survival— her expendability had just risen a few notches in his mind.

If it comes down to me or her, I'm not sacrificing myself for some kid killer.

He crouched behind a tree, fifty yards from the concrete building. The raised voices had made him stop his pursuit. It had sounded like they were squabbling like children over what was inside the concrete structure.

This had come as no surprise. Half an hour ago, the man and two women hadn't noticed him through the window when they'd entered the hardware store. They had been too desperate to get inside, and the axe had almost made them pay for their frantic moves. He'd watched the whole thing, arms folded, baffled about how a group of adults could be so utterly stupid.

How have they not figured this out by now?

But it wouldn't be long before something else got them.

A smile stretched across his face as he watched them disappear through the forest. A few years back, he'd watched a teenage girl do the same thing, wandering into a remote area without knowing he was silently following her, already fantasizing about the sexual violence that he was about to inflict.

Once confident of the group's continued direction, and that they were far enough away to not hear him, he rose to a standing position and headed toward the bunker to check out the mutilated corpse.

Each second brought him closer to the bloodied body. Each step got him more and more turned on by what he was about to see.

Another weak member of society falling prey to this giant, obvious snare.

To him, there were two types of people in this world. Hunters and prey. These people were all prey, destined for death. They were born to die.

He leaned down to examine the serrated teeth of the bear trap that had crushed the corpse's leg.

The man raised his eyebrows at the torn flesh around the exposed intestines. It was brutal work, a touch barbaric for even him, but it saved him the effort.

He casually booted the corpse in the head. A spray of blood exploded out of its open mouth and spattered the nearby ferns.

The man headed across to the concrete bunker, retracing the steps of the group through the disturbed undergrowth.

Inside the building, one of them had ripped newspaper clippings from the wall. It seemed like a pointless gesture, considering that their end had already been dictated by a mind more powerful than their own.

It was all so . . .

The man resisted the urge to play with himself.

He didn't want the three victims to get too far ahead. There would be enough time to get this out of his system after this whole thing was over.

Maybe tomorrow morning.

And the chase had so far given him enough of a thrill.

He headed back outside into the freezing wind.

Turned away from the town and followed in the direction of the group.

After a few minutes, he detected the sound of voices. Distant figures, struggling to make progress.

This was a safe distance to observe and study.

Perhaps witness one of their deaths in real time.

Nothing would give me greater joy . . .

There would be a single winner in this game. And he had already proven many times that when it came to a matchup between himself and these types of people, he was hands-down unbeatable.

18

Jess strode through the forest, moving fast in the lead to try to get some warmth into her body. The other reason for putting some distance between her and the remaining bunch was to avoid Trinity. She had been repulsed by the other woman's story behind her being here. The crime was reprehensible.

And she got away with it . . .

With murdering a child while drunk-driving.

Trinity's subsequent lack of ownership of her crime was intolerable. It made Jess's blood boil.

The very essence of an ethical life was owning up to everything. The good and the bad. So many people are not honest with themselves, about who they *really* are. Trinity would never find peace in denial, but that was her choice and she would have to live with it. Or perhaps die because of it.

Jess had her own issues to deal with. The sturdy boots and thick hiking socks that had kept her feet warm were starting to lose their battle against the harsh winter. Her toes felt like blocks of ice. She had her hands retracted in her coat sleeves, the screwdriver in her shivering right one.

The survivors all needed some respite from the elements, and the impending dangers. Old Forge and the surrounding area had rapidly become a slaughterhouse. The lifeless trees looming over the group, with their skeletal branches, matched the dark mood of Eddie's and Trinity's faces.

Only they could set themselves free. And the chances were slim, given that they had no idea what they were truly facing.

This town is our reckoning.

Trinity picked up the pace and pulled level with Jess, leaving Eddie trailing behind. "I noticed the way you glared at me before. I'm not a monster, you know?"

"I never said you were."

"You looked at me like I was a piece of shit."

Again, Jess thought, *the selfish attitude.* Despite the hole everyone had found themselves in, Trinity had an uncanny way of always belittling others and making everything about herself. But Jess had patience; she had needed it throughout her life to battle different types of adversity. This was a massive test of her temperament.

"That kid wasn't my fault," Trinity continued. "Besides, I barely drank that afternoon. And who lets their kid play outside alone anyway? Seriously? No one bothered to blame the mom for what—"

"SHUT UP, TRINITY," Jess snapped, cutting her off. She stopped and faced the other woman. "You want to know what I think?"

"Yeah."

"I think you've never taken responsibility for any of the damage you've caused in your life. I think you're selfish, narcissistic, reckless. And yes, a total piece of shit."

Trinity stopped, stunned by the sudden bluntness.

"And I think you *deserve* to be here," Jess added as a final flourish. "We all do . . ." she added quietly, under her breath.

She turned back ahead and continued her march through the forest, leaving Trinity behind to deal with the fallout.

Jess internally kicked herself. She was pissed for losing her cool, but enough was enough. She couldn't contain her anger any longer.

Whatever happens to Trinity, she's got it coming.

A few minutes later, under a thicker part of the forest canopy, Jess spotted an unnatural depression in the ground.

Eddie must have seen it too. He barreled past, and stopped by the side of a trail that wound between the trees into the distance. It was a few feet wide, with multiple footprints in the dirt.

"Our captors must have come this way," he said, angling his weapon down at the prints. "I mean, who else could it have been?"

"So we avoid it?" Trinity asked in a quiet voice.

"Are you kidding? It could be our way out. If we come across them, we fight."

"What if they're armed?"

"If they were armed," Jess said, "don't you think they could have just killed us by now?"

Trinity let out a dismissive grunt. "Or those assholes want to see if we got caught in their traps first. They are playing with us. We'll be carrying a knife to a gunfight—"

"We're following the trail," Eddie cut in sternly. "The alternatives are freezing to death in the forest or going back to the church. You got any better ideas?"

His words carried anxiety, though also stern resolve that appealed to Jess's own survival instinct. She had little doubt that Eddie would see tomorrow. Trinity and the shadowy figure that bolted from the church? Probably not.

Jess and Trinity half-jogged to keep up with Eddie's stride as he powered along the trail. After a few sweaty minutes, an unnatural gray barrier appeared in the distance, carving a straight line between the trees.

"What the hell?" Eddie blurted.

Jess also stopped to try to make sense of what she was seeing. "Is that . . ." she said, squinting, "a wall?"

They continued forward. Soon, the trees gave way to a long, cleared stretch of land. A massive cinder block wall stretched from left to right, cutting a path directly through the forest as far as the eye could see. It rose at least ten feet high and was topped with four rows of menacing barbed wire.

A low electric hum came from the top of the huge structure.

"Is this some kind of perimeter fence?" Trinity asked.

Eddie nodded. "To keep us in and anyone else out."

"It must circle the entire town," Jess added.

"No doubt."

"How the fuck do we get over it?" Trinity hissed.

"You hear that hum?" Eddie asked. "This thing is electrified. There's no going over it."

"So what the hell do we do?"

Eddie peered along a trail that ran parallel to the cinder blocks. "There's gotta be a way in and out. A gate of some kind. Look at the footprints. They follow the wall to the right."

"That's our answer," Jess said. "Let's see where they lead."

The group swapped apprehensive glances. Jess also detected a hint of excitement in Trinity's and Eddie's eyes. This was the nearest they had come to finding the possible edge of this nightmare.

Eddie led the way along the meandering trail under the shadow of the wall. Tree stumps peppered the path between the perimeter and the forest, showing that a wide area had been purposefully cleared for construction. The large number of fresh footprints also made it obvious that this route had been used recently.

Soon, a wide gap in the wall appeared as it curved to the west.

Jess, Eddie, and Trinity slowly approached, glancing in all directions for any signs of movement. Step by step they closed in, each treading carefully to avoid kicking a rock, snapping a twig, or triggering a booby trap.

Eventually, Eddie reached a set of chain-link gates, equally as tall as the wall and robustly built. The sound of an electric current buzzed loudly from the galvanized steel wires. He peered around the wall's edge toward the outside world.

"Whaddya see?" Trinity murmured.

"A house."

"What?"

Trinity and Jess rapidly stooped to take a look, surprised at the sight in the distance.

A rolling field was immediately behind the gates, shrouded in a low layer of mist. A dirt road cut directly from the gates to a farmhouse, the quintessential old-style American dwelling with a white facade, an ornate porch, a series of surrounding barns, a mini-farm, and vintage tractors and cars inside a huge open garage.

Smoke belched from the brick chimney and coiled into the murky gray sky, suggesting somebody was home, and likely cooking.

"Look," Eddie said, pointing to the left of the house. A concrete road disappeared into the mist on the other side. "We find a way over, steal a car, and make a break for it."

"Steal a car?" Trinity asked.

"I wasn't a saint in my past."

"No shit. That's why you're here."

He scowled. "I wouldn't go there if I were in your shoes."

For the next few minutes, they observed the quiet farm and strategized about how to get over or through the fence. Trinity suggested finding and smashing the electricity box, which sounded like the worst idea. Eddie wanted to use a log as a battering ram, figuring the wood would insulate them from the electric current.

A strong gust of wind blew from the direction of the farmhouse, momentarily disturbing the mist.

Jess looked to the other side of the gate. A security camera had been positioned to see directly down on the group's side of the gate, its weak red light only just visible. "We're being watched, guys," she said.

"Goddamn it," Eddie spat. "It's now or never."

"No shit," Trinity said, staring toward the property. "Take a look."

Jess followed her gaze to the front door.

It had opened, and two figures were heading across the field, straight toward the gate. They moved at a slow pace, nothing to suggest they meant any trouble. From here, it looked like neither carried a weapon.

"Maybe they can help us," Trinity whispered.

"I wouldn't bet on it," Eddie said. "This is the entrance to the compound, and that's their house. Or do you think these are nice, homey folks, and there's a different entry point with another house full of murderers?"

"Fair enough. What do we do?"

"They already know we're here," Jess said. "Might as well see what they want."

The two people, wearing thick coats and scarves, shuffled over the snow-covered ground. As they approached the gate and emerged clearly from the mist, Eddie turned to Jess and whispered to her, his voice barely audible.

"Jess, it's them. The old couple that kidnapped me . . ."

19

Eddie almost had to pinch himself to believe this reality. Sure, it came as no surprise to see his abductors. But for them to have set this whole thing up and carry out these acts? He didn't believe that for a second. For a start, the old man didn't have the strength to bash someone's face in with a heavy log. And he certainly couldn't go toe-to-toe with Tank in the church, like the athletic shadowy figure he had witnessed during the fight.

The old man gazed at him through glassy eyes. He looked like a clean-shaven version of Donald Sutherland. The old woman, he thought, resembled Betty White. She inspected each one of them in turn with a look of pity, as if being shown a lineup of inmates on death row.

"Hello, Eddie, Trinity, and Jessica," the old man said, breaking the ice. "My name is George, and this is my wife, Dorothy."

"What the fuck do you want from us?" Trinity yelled.

"Please, mind your language," Dorothy said softly, like a matronly grandmother gently chiding a child.

"My goddamn language? Are you insane?"

The old man shook his head in disappointment. "Don't task us, young lady. We don't want anything from you. Our job is just about done."

"*Just about?*" Eddie asked. "What does that mean?"

The old man locked eyes with him. "I believe you know what that means."

The potential implications of the old man's response sent shivers down Eddie's spine.

"George, Dorothy," Jess said calmly. "May I ask why we're here?"

George considered her question for a few moments. "In all my years, there is one certainty I've come to realize: It is impossible to escape one's past."

He wrapped his arm around his wife, to warm her from the cold. "You are precisely where you each need to be, wouldn't you agree?"

"The two of you are sick," Trinity shot back.

"I assure you, young lady," Dorothy said. "It gives us no pleasure seeing you inside this cage."

"Which is why," George added, "we'll be opening this gate tomorrow, Christmas morning, at sunrise. If you are here, you will be free to go."

Eddie frowned. "I don't get it. What's the catch?"

"There is no catch," George said. "Christmas is a time for hope, not recompense. If you are here at sunrise, you can walk out without consequence."

Eddie shook his head in disbelief. "Look, old man. If I walk out of here tomorrow, there are gonna be consequences for *you*."

George pulled Dorothy even closer to stop her shivering. "Perhaps," he replied, lost in thought. "Perhaps."

For a tense moment, everyone eyed one another.

"Until tomorrow then," George said.

With that, the old couple headed back toward their farmhouse.

When the old man reached the doorway, he turned back.

"Oh, one last thing," he called out, his voice weak. "The temperature drops to minus ten tonight. Be very careful now, you hear?"

George escorted Dorothy back into their farmhouse, leaving a shocked Eddie, Trinity, and Jess behind in their frozen prison.

20

The group stood in silence as a few different lights from the farmhouse flicked on and off. For some reason, the temperature outside felt colder since the old man's dire warning. The agonizing ache in Eddie's limbs had extended to his shoulders and back. His shiver had become uncontrollable; he needed to get blood pumping through his body again.

One thing was certain in his mind, though. He wouldn't survive a night outside. None of them would. They had to find refuge, and find it fast.

"What the fuck was that?" Trinity asked. "There's no way they're letting us walk out of here tomorrow morning, is there?"

Eddie considered the bizarre exchange with the elderly couple before responding. "Call me crazy, but I believe they're sincere. Tomorrow morning, we can go free. That is, *if* we're still alive."

"But clearly, they don't think we will be," Jess said.

"Exactly right. Which means they are not the ones doing the killing."

"Which also means there's someone else inside this prison with us."

"Or multiple killers," Trinity said. "So, what the fuck do we do? Search the perimeter for a way out?"

"I don't think that'll work," Jess replied. "Clearly, they've thought that through. I doubt they missed something."

"We're in the killing fields," Eddie said somberly, shaking his head at how his life had led to this.

Trinity let out a frustrated grunt. "So back to the original question. What the fuck do we do now?"

"Shelter," Eddie said. "We hole up somewhere until the morning. Wait this out."

"You're not seriously considering going back to the church, are you? Is that really your plan? We'd be easy targets."

"True. But I can't help thinking that we're missing something."

"Like what?"

"I don't know."

Old Forge had no clear narrative. No clear way forward. All it had was death and fear. Eddie struggled to think of a plan. Or even the best direction of travel from here.

"That satellite dish looked brand-new, right?" Jess asked.

"Yeah," Eddie said. "But there was nothing in the concrete building."

"Well, not nothing." Jess shot a look at Trinity. "But let's think this through. The satellite dish *has* to lead somewhere. If not into that building, then somewhere else."

Eddie nodded. "I follow."

"We track the cable, see where it goes."

"Good call. Let's do it."

As he had no better idea.

The group trekked back along the meandering path that hugged the internal perimeter. Every few seconds, Eddie switched his focus from the ground to the surrounding area, conscious that someone could jump him at any second.

Behind him, footsteps crunched on the trail's frosty surface. The two women followed briskly, perhaps buoyed that they might make a discovery. Maybe find something that they weren't supposed to see. Turn the tables in their favor. Barricade themselves inside somewhere until morning.

Eddie slowed to a stop as he neared the structure. He crouched behind a tree and encouraged Jess and Trinity over. The group's earlier footprints were still visible on the ground, meaning he wouldn't step into another bear trap.

"What you waiting for?" Trinity wheezed between deep breaths.

"A goddamn boulder to chase us. Or a tree to fall on our heads. Who the fuck knows with this place."

"Look at the right edge of the wall," Jess said.

A thick black cable ran from the dish to the battered gutter, then along the wall to the ground. Eddie had incorrectly assumed earlier that the cable ran into the concrete building, but now, upon closer inspection, it was obvious that it led in a different direction, away from the structure.

"But where does it go?" Trinity murmured.

"That's the question. Let's give it another minute."

Eddie surveyed the forest.

And for a second, the area gave him an odd sense of déjà vu. The strangest of recollections at a moment of immense danger. He remembered the first time he had stolen something. As a sixteen-year-old in Fort Drum, he and his buddies had heard that Old Man Visco kept a stash of booze in his remote cabin. They'd scoped the place out. Concluded nobody was home and smashed a window to get inside. The alcohol was nonexistent, though they did manage to find a couple of porn mags with stuck-together pages and a flashlight.

Not exactly the mother lode.

But the teenagers had talked about it for weeks. He could

remember the rush. The unbeatable feeling of having taken something that didn't belong to him. The rush from *taking*.

Eddie silently shook his head. He wondered if that was the moment when he hit the slippery slope—got the appetite for illegally acquiring things—that had led to the walled-off terror of this replica of Old Forge.

Back in the present, he crept from behind the tree and made his way over to the concrete building. Greg's body was still in the same location, though his head had flopped to the side. His vacant eyes stared at Eddie as he approached.

He reached the building's side wall. Wiped frost away from the cable with his coat sleeve. Traced it down to the ground, where it disappeared under a layer of pine needles.

For a moment, he dreaded the thought of the cable being buried under the frozen ground. He scraped the needles away with his boot, and a small wave of relief washed over him.

The cable had been concealed by a thin layer of the forest floor, and it headed in the direction of a small clearing.

"Grab it," Jess encouraged.

Eddie pulled his sleeves down to protect his hands. He grabbed the bottom end of the cable in a two-handed grip and heaved.

After three hefty pulls, several yards of cable rose from the ground, throwing up pine needles and dead leaves. Eddie slipped the black plastic sheathing through his hands, advanced a few steps, and ripped it up again.

Jess and Trinity excitedly moved by his side, willing him to keep going.

Eventually, after traveling roughly fifty feet from the building, the cable twanged rigid next to a disturbed pile of leaves and branches.

"Looks like someone covered something up," Trinity said.

Eddie looked over his shoulder. "You don't say."

He and Jess threw the bigger branches to the side. Next, they started kicking away the rest of the natural debris.

Eddie went to step across to a mound of needles. His right foot thudded against solid wood and a dull echo returned from below. For a moment, he stood fixed to the spot, half-expecting to hurtle downward into a pit filled with spikes.

Nothing happened.

He tapped the heel of his boot downward.

"What is it?" Trinity whispered.

Eddie used the side of his boot to brush the remaining leaves and needles away from a varnished door. It was square-shaped, roughly three feet by three feet, set in concrete. Jess finished the job by stooping down to clear away the natural debris that had snagged around a stainless-steel latch. It was the type that opened from the inside out, so it was impossible to tell if anyone was below.

Eddie looked in all directions, sucking in deep breaths. The distance they had traveled, the bitterly painful cold, and the lack of food were weighing heavily on him. Trepidation also fought hard against his minor exhilaration at the find.

He refused to get his hopes up just yet.

"They concealed it for a reason," Jess said, "Let's find out why."

Trinity dragged her back by the arm. "Not so fast. They might be inside. This could be where they've been watching us from."

"If that's true, then they already know we're out here. Right?"

"We're going in," Eddie said firmly. "The satellite dish tells us there's electricity down there. Maybe heat. Maybe food. If we have to fight for it, I'm more than game."

He knelt next to the latch. Grabbed the cold metal and twisted it up.

The next move was sliding the bolt open.

Eddie peered up at the women. "On the count of three we go in, no matter what."

The group held their breath, not knowing what . . . or whom . . . they would face inside the hatch.

"One . . ."

"Two . . ."

"Three . . ."

21

The bolt let out a metallic screech as it slid open along the rail. Eddie cringed at the piercing sound, which undoubtedly carried a long way through the forest, potentially revealing their location to their captors.

If anyone was tracking them, they'd certainly heard the screech. However, the luxury of time had long disappeared. There was simply no other choice but to find refuge from the biting temperature.

He looked up. "Ready?"

"Go for it," Jess said.

Eddie slowly lifted the wooden boards, allowing natural light to flood into a ten-foot concrete shaft. A ladder had been screwed to the wall. At the bottom, on the right side, a steel door with a wheel lock blocked another entrance.

A knot of apprehension formed in his stomach.

Trinity and Jess peered into the drop.

"Whaddaya think?" he asked.

"Your guess is as good as mine," Jess said. "So . . . who wants to go first?"

"I guess I'll do it," Eddie said apprehensively. "Keep a lookout, in case you need to save my ass again."

"You got it."

Eddie lowered himself a few feet down the ladder, carefully stepping on each rung. The fact that the shaft had been concealed made him hopeful that he was not walking into another trap.

He jumped down the last few feet.

His boots splashed in a shallow pool of water, showering the surrounding walls. He immediately turned to face the door. Its light blue metallic paint looked spotless. The wheel lock made it appear like a submarine entrance. He grabbed the chrome circle and twisted it counterclockwise. Much to his surprise, it spun with well-oiled ease, whirring at smooth speed.

The locking mechanism thudded.

Eddie raised his screwdriver. He shoved the door open a couple of inches.

Warmth instantly rushed out of the gap.

His heart skipped a beat. It was the first positive thing he'd experienced since the woodstove in the church, which seemed like a million years ago at this point.

Eddie detected a strange chemical scent and immediately held his breath. His initial thought was poison gas, but he quickly ruled it out. His best guess was cleaning fluid, or a type of fuel.

"I'm going in," he whispered up.

He slipped through the gap in the door and entered near darkness. A soft glow came from an adjoining room, highlighting dark shapes in front of him. A quiet hum filled the air like a working fridge or an HVAC system.

For a few seconds, it felt like his skin was actively sucking in the heat. With a determined, shaky step, he went in farther. Eddie groped his fingers along the wall until he found the reassuring shape of a light switch. He flicked it up.

An overhead striplight burst on. It strobed a few times before turning solid.

He squinted at the sudden brightness, looking with some disbelief at the quirky scene in the brightly lit room.

The place was the size of an average living room, with white-painted walls. On a central table, a miniature version of the town had been built. On first inspection, it perfectly mirrored what he had seen, down to the Christmas decorations in the store windows and the painted decorations on the merry-go-round's horses. Someone had gone to a lot of time and effort to create this chilling little masterpiece.

But a strange, unrewarded effort. The type that brought about personal satisfaction, but one that could likely never be widely discussed. Maybe similar to a SEAL operation, but only more depraved.

"What do you see, Eddie?" Jess called out.

"Is it safe?" Trinity shouted down.

He moved back outside the hatch and looked up. "As far as I can tell, yes. It's . . . well . . . I don't know what to make of it. Let me check more. Gimme a sec."

"I can feel heat coming up," Trinity said, shivering. "You think I'm waiting?"

She immediately clambered down the ladder. Jess came straight after and closed the latch door above. While they descended, Eddie did a fast scan of the space to make sure no one was waiting to surprise them.

Trinity and Jess came in through the doorway, looked around the chamber, and saw the bizarre town model in the middle of the room.

Their expressions matched Eddie's initial thoughts.

"What the hell?" Trinity gasped.

"Right?" Eddie replied.

"Are we alone?" Jess asked.

Eddie nodded. "It seems that way. There's another room over there. But first . . ."

He shut the door and spun the wheel. It locked with a deep clunk.

Trinity spun to face him. "You're sealing us in?"

"No, I'm locking others out. If they try to open the door, we'll hear them. It'll buy us a few seconds to prepare."

"Smart idea," Jess said.

She circled the central table, inspecting different areas of the model town, examining the intricate buildings and streets in evident curiosity. Eddie savored the warmth while she gazed at the tiny details.

"Whaddaya think?" he asked.

"About the model? It's nearly perfect."

"Nearly?"

"I seem to recall the false front of the cobbler's store collapsing yesterday."

He gave her a thin smile. "You're right."

Jess leaned over the model. She flicked over the miniature front of the cobbler's store. "That's better."

Eddie turned his focus to the adjoining back room. The sound of a consistent electric hum became louder as he neared. He headed through the doorway into a stranger place than the first room.

It had been fashioned as a high-tech surveillance hub. A bank of eight television monitors were fixed to the wall above a modern office console. They displayed images of different parts of the town and various camera angles of inside the chapel, the hardware store, the town hall, the inn, the saloon, the merry-go-round. Every few seconds, each monitor switched to footage of another area of the town. The entire place must have been rigged with hidden security cameras.

It made him think that the very obvious camera in the pharmacy—with its blinking red light—had been purposefully positioned in plain sight. A way to tell the hostages that they were being constantly watched.

One screen displayed an overhead shot of the latch door. They were clearly recorded entering from above a few minutes earlier.

But from the looks of it, there were no cameras inside the hatch. For the moment, Eddie, Trinity, and Jess were the all-seeing gods of the replica of Old Forge. And that gave him a crumb of extra confidence.

"We got some *Truman Show* shit in here," Eddie called out. He turned to check out the rest of the surveillance hub.

A blue glow came from a sterile-looking photographic table on the other side of the room. Lights beneath the table illuminated an array of neatly placed files and photographs. Eddie took a quick look before heading through the next doorway. The first thing he noticed was a picture of himself. It looked like it had been downloaded from his Instagram page, a profile picture of him posing outside a haunted house in Niagara Falls three years prior.

It set his mind racing.

If this was planned, how long have they been after me?

How long have I been tracked?

These questions would have to wait. He strode into the final space in the underground complex.

A large generator hummed in the corner. It had a bank of backup batteries and four enormous fuel cylinders. Enough to keep a full-sized house running for several days. Or a killer's lair for weeks at a time.

Eddie did a search of a small kitchenette. A single mug and plate had been left on a drying rack. There was a magnetic calendar on the wall, with a black circle placed over yesterday's date. He pulled open a fridge containing cold cuts, fruit, bread, cheese slices, and six bottles of mineral water.

He reached for the closest one. But a voice in his head screamed for him to stop. The memory of the acid burning through Tank's esophagus in the church came rushing back to complement the warning.

It wasn't worth the risk, despite his ravenous stomach. At least, for now.

Eddie made his way back into the surveillance hub. Jess looked up at him from the photographic table. "Have you seen this?"

"Not yet, apart from my mug shot."

"It's got pictures and descriptions of *everyone.*"

Eddie examined his file more closely. It contained plenty of derogatory details about him, amounting to a character assassination. It highlighted all of his bad points, had interview quotes from a supposed friend, and at the bottom featured a full psychological breakdown of his expected behavior under duress.

"What the . . ." he said, scanning the documents in disbelief. "Well, apparently, I'm unreliable, untrustworthy, my buddy thinks I'm an asshole, and I'd act selfishly if I got in a jam. Oh yeah, it also says I'd probably sell my granny down the river for five bucks."

"You don't seem that way to me," Jess said.

Eddie sat on a corner of the table. The truth hurt, and he realized that at this point, he had nothing to hide. "Sadly," he said, "this thing ain't wrong. I used to be just what it says, still am in many ways, but I've been trying. I gotta believe people can change. What does it say about you?"

"I haven't got that far yet."

They spent the next few minutes identifying who they knew from the photographs and scanning their files. Each criminal had sections describing their strengths, weaknesses, and psychological profiles.

None of it was flattering.

Trinity's hit-and-run accident and divisiveness in a group setting. Tank's rampant drug history and impulsiveness. Greg's multiple con jobs and disruptive behavior.

The profiles were dead-on accurate.

How much planning did this take?

"Where's Trinity?" he asked.

"Going through the file cabinets."

"What do you make of all this?"

"We were tracked, studied, chosen," Jess said. "This is a planned hunt. None of it is a coincidence."

Eddie peered around the hub. "Who went to this amount of trouble?"

"That's the million-dollar question, isn't it?"

Trinity hustled into the room and slammed down a pile of files on the table. "You guys need to see this, now."

"What's in them?" Eddie asked.

"This isn't the first goddamn time!"

"Wait . . . What do you mean?"

"All this shit we're going through, all this death and torture." Trinity shook her head in disbelief. "This has happened *every year* since 2010."

ddie stared down at the files. The blue cardboard had slightly faded on the earlier ones. Dates had been stamped on the front, confirming what Trinity had said. He fanned them out and flipped open to the oldest.

It contained a final report on the front page, detailing how all six captives had been killed in 2010.

The first was stabbed through the chest. The second was strangled. Third, bludgeoned. Fourth, hypothermia. Fifth, slit throat. And the sixth person was shot. Eddie didn't recognize any of their names, but all had lived in Upstate New York, and all had a criminal past.

A creeping sense of dread came over him as he leafed through the 2017 summary. Back then, six victims had been brought to the town, all around Christmastime, and their deaths were far more elaborate than the original bloodbath in 2010.

One victim was burned at the stake, another drowned, one was electrocuted, another poisoned, one skinned alive, and the final victim was hung from the inn's second-story window.

The last killing included a photo of a dead woman, her hands tied behind her back, a burlap sack over her head, a noose around her neck as she hung several feet from the snowy ground. It also appeared that her tendons had been severed just above her heels.

The killers had clearly honed their craft over the years, with horrifyingly creative results.

"What . . . the . . . fuck," he murmured.

The matter-of-fact recording of the details on a typed page, ruthless and methodical, made his blood run cold.

Matters of life and death, boiled down to an Excel spreadsheet.

Jess and Trinity stared in disbelief at the other files.

He grabbed the second-to-last one—2023—off the table and flipped it open.

He puffed out a strong breath after reading about the first two deaths. The first victim, Brian Luger, had been knocked semiconscious with half a brick, then had his nostrils and mouth superglued shut. The second, Jenny Beekman, was suffocated in an airtight steel drum with a clear lid. Apparently, she'd lasted for three minutes, desperately clawing at the plastic with her press-on nails, to no avail.

Eddie turned his attention back to the current file, 2024. He froze in fear seeing his name on the list, written so matter-of-factly.

Eddie Parker.

His name was his death sentence, but the means of execution had not been filled in yet.

He read the remaining names.

Jessica Kane.

Trinity Jackson.

Greg Fisher.

Tank.

And then, a name he didn't recognize.

"Who's Damien Hurst?" he said under his breath.

Trinity looked up from another file. "Huh?"

"The list of names for our *hunt.* There's an extra one here: Damien Hurst."

"Could be Tank?" Jess said.

"No, he's in here under his pseudonym."

The women moved to his side and peered down at Damien Hurst's photo.

Jess frowned. "Maybe he's the guy who fled the church?"

Eddie nodded in agreement. "Must be."

"Wait a second," Trinity said. "Damien Hurst. I know that name."

She sifted through the files to the present year and found the information on him. "Yep, I've heard all about this sick son of a bitch. He's notorious."

"Who is he?" Jess asked.

"A serial rapist from Syracuse, murdered a few of his victims afterward. He was thought to be on the run."

"Don't think he'll be running much anymore," Eddie said, shaking his head. "He has to be the guy whose skull was crushed in the forest. He must have run out of the church and been the first to get picked off."

"He deserved worse, trust me. I think he raped four or five women total."

"Seven," Jess said. "I remember the case too."

"Well, good riddance then," Eddie said. "I gotta be honest here, though, I don't quite see how my crimes are equal to this asshole's."

"You sure about that?" Jess asked. "I think that depends on your point of view, doesn't it?"

Eddie considered this for a moment. "Yeah, I suppose it does."

She looked toward the back of the hub. "What did you find back there?"

"There's some kind of power supply, and a kitchenette. Check it out."

Eddie led them through the doorway into the dimly lit area. Trinity headed straight for the fridge and checked out the contents.

"I wouldn't if I were you," he said.

She froze, likely remembering the incident in the church.

At the opposite end of the room, Jess studied the generator and bank of batteries. She moved to an odd-looking metal box on the wall.

"What do you think is inside this?" she asked.

"Only one way to find out," Eddie replied.

She hesitated, maybe sensing it could be a trap. But to Eddie, the group had already established that this was a place that wasn't meant for them. They were never supposed to find this.

"Well," Jess said. "I suppose it's my turn to gamble."

She delicately creaked the box open and leaned in closer. "Come here," she said to Eddie.

"What is it?"

"Look." She ran her finger across two rows of labeled circuit breakers. "A circuit board. Looks like it controls the electricity for the entire town. There's a switch for each building. The streetlights, the Christmas tree, the merry-go-round. They're all on timers."

The breaker for the tree was on, explaining it as the only visible electricity in the town. But the label over the last switch gave Eddie a butterfly of excitement. "Access tunnel?!" he blurted out.

"What?"

"Right there, the last one. It says 'access tunnel.'"

"You're thinking it's a way in and out?" Jess asked.

"It's gotta be. How else did they get all of us in here? How else are they traveling undetected? That tunnel could be our ticket out of here."

"But where is it?"

"Trinity, get those blueprints again."

Trinity grabbed a large, rolled-up piece of paper from the desk. She unfurled the document, which stretched from her head to her shoes, revealing a highly detailed blueprint of the replica of Old Forge.

Eddie approached for a closer inspection. He couldn't make out specifics without better lighting. "Let's spread it out on the photographic table."

Back in the hub, Trinity and Eddie stretched the schematic across the glowing surface. Once the paper was flattened, every detail became legible.

The schematic showed the date that each building had been constructed over the last decade. The first victims in the town would have come across a sparse version of Old Forge, with only three bare-bones buildings, compared with the dozen or so inhabiting the town now.

It also displayed plans for future buildings. A blacksmith, a butcher shop, and a liquor store. With every passing year, the town grew larger and larger.

"There," Jess said, pointing down at the town square.

A newsstand lay to the right of the Christmas tree. Next to it, in faded letters, someone had written *Access Tunnel—2017.*

"That's it!" Eddie exclaimed. "Right underneath the fake newsstand in town. Betcha it's a way out of here!"

"Could be," Jess said. "Could not be."

Her reality check quickly suppressed Eddie's initial exuberance.

Dammit. She's right.

"We have a choice to make," Jess added. "On the one hand, we're here in this bunker, alone, in a defendable position. It's warm, and there's food, but there's no way to know if we can eat it. We *could* just wait here until morning and then head back to the gate."

"But that's making a huge assumption," Trinity said. "That the old couple was telling the truth and will just let us out."

"Exactly. Or we head to the access tunnel to see if we can slip out of town under the cover of darkness."

Eddie considered both scenarios. The chill had finally left his body, and it was difficult to consider leaving their temporary refuge. They had a realistic shot at survival here. But then he looked back at the chart with his name on it, the means of his death still not filled in.

"Here's my take," he said after considering everything. "We stay here, we're dead. Seeing all this—the charts, the psychological breakdowns of each of us, the scale of their preparations—it's become very clear to me that no one is just *letting* us out of here. So I, for one, say we take fate into our own hands. If we're gonna die either way, let's go out swinging. Fuck 'em."

"So?" Jess asked. "What's your choice?"

"The tunnel," he said. "We make a break for it, and get the hell out of this godforsaken place."

23

E ddie received nods of agreement from Trinity and Jess. That was all he needed to promptly return to the breaker box in the other room. He found the switch for the access tunnel and turned the power on.

Let's hope this does the trick.

He jogged back to the first room and grabbed the wheel lock door. "Ready to freeze your asses off again?"

Trinity and Jess headed over to his side.

"Okay, let's move." Eddie spun the wheel to open the lock, and thrust open the latch door. The subzero temperature hit him hard, and he momentarily lost his breath. But the blast of warmth had invigorated him. He pushed through the frigid air, clambering back up the ladder to the ground-level darkness.

For a moment, he wondered if the group had made the right choice. Perhaps it would have been smarter to shelter in place until morning. But he knew no cavalry was coming to their rescue, and after seeing everything in this bunker, it was clear the elderly couple could not be taken at their word.

We stay, we die.

Eddie smirked at his next thought. *We move, we probably still die.*

He took in the dark surroundings of the forest. Snowflakes fell between the gaps in trees and had started to form a fresh layer.

Thankfully, the blizzard-like conditions of yesterday had not returned, though wind whipped between the trees, throwing up thin clouds of snow. He wondered how the day had passed so fast. How darkness had returned so fast. It seemed like they had left the church only a few hours ago.

Eddie searched the immediate area for any signs of a predator, human or otherwise. He signaled the all clear to the women below, and they ascended the ladder to join him.

"Lead the way, Eddie," Trinity whispered.

It seemed to him that an odd acceptance, dare he say camaraderie, had begun to form in the group. Perhaps it was seeing all their sins and deeply held secrets laid out so precisely in the bunker. Perhaps it was the now full understanding of the danger they faced. Whatever it was, they were in this together. Even Trinity was acting like a team player.

Eddie led the way and headed through the trees toward the town at a slow pace. They passed Greg's mangled corpse, now frozen, with a light covering of snow on top of it. They passed through the small clearing where they had first spotted the bear, and into the denser part of the forest.

Every twig or branch that snagged on Eddie's coat made his heart race even faster. It only took a few minutes for his hands and feet to numb. He pushed any shreds of self-pity to the back of his mind. Determination carried him forward.

Soon, they passed the battered body of Damien Hurst, his face crushed under a rock. The skin on his hands and exposed stomach looked milk-bottle white, with dark blotches underneath. A small saving grace was the ice-cold weather. It allowed the group to avoid having to suffer the stench of human decomposition.

Eddie had experienced that stomach-churning smell once in his life. His estranged dad, Billy Parker, had been an alcoholic who lived alone in a dilapidated cabin in the middle of nowhere. When nobody had heard from Billy for two weeks—even the local liquor store—Eddie investigated. He found his father's charred corpse in his stained old La-Z-Boy, fire damage all around the interior of the cabin. He'd likely passed out drunk while holding a lit cigarette, and suffered one of the worse fates imaginable. And the smell . . .

He'd never forget that smell.

It was the type of inglorious end that Eddie wished on no man or woman.

Ironic that Eddie's fate might end up very similar, if he couldn't get beyond the walls of his cage. He imagined his body being found, two weeks later, by God knows who. His frozen skin, tinted bluish gray from the elements, likely ripped into a thousand pieces by scavengers in the forest, desperate for food to last the winter.

Or perhaps . . . his body would never be found, would be buried in lime or dissolved with hydrochloric acid by his captors once their hunt was complete.

The morbid thoughts were too much to bear, and he snapped back to the mission at hand.

The town slowly appeared between the tall pine trees.

Eddie paused behind one of them.

He considered the best way to reach the newsstand. Going straight down the street could make them sitting ducks. However, circumnavigating the town would delay their escape attempt further.

Jess crept to his side. "What are you thinking?"

"Every choice has its risks. Don't know which is best."

"Every action in life has its risks." Jess looked around the immediate area as light snow continued to fall. "No footprints."

"Nothing to indicate someone is onto us."

"Precisely."

"Then, we head straight to the newsstand, and we move fast."

Suddenly, the streetlights along Old Forge's main road thumped on in sequence, bathing every storefront in a yellow glow. The Christmas decorations attached to the middle of the posts burst to life. Neon snowmen. Santa. Reindeers. Elves. Gingerbread men.

Inside the stores, lights punched on all at once.

At the far end of the square, the merry-go-round lit up, dazzling wreaths on every support. Multicolored bulbs flashed around the top section. They reflected off the mirrored center pole, making the elaborately painted horses shimmer.

Before Eddie could say anything, a series of speakers crackled across the town. A moment later, an old version of "Santa Claus Is Coming to Town" boomed out. The singer's voice slurred and changed speed, like the track was being played on a warped record.

The lyrics scared him more than the sound or the weather. They carried a sinister message that seemed perfect for this remote town.

> . . . *He's making a list*
> *And checking it twice*
> *He's gonna find out who's naughty and nice*
> *Santa Claus is coming to town*
> . . . *He sees you when you're sleeping*
> *He knows when you're awake*
> *He knows if you've been bad or good*
> *So be good for goodness' sake*

In the distance, a rocket firework fizzed into the air. It exploded beneath the snow-packed clouds, letting out a glittering sea of green and red sparkles.

The replica of Old Forge had suddenly roared to festive life.

"What the actual fuck?" Trinity whispered.

"Maybe they saw us coming," Eddie said.

"I'm not so sure," Jess said. "Remember, all those breakers were on timers."

"And they just happened to go off when we reached the edge of town? Seems like one hell of a coincidence."

"The town didn't light up like this last night," Trinity added.

"It wasn't Christmas Eve," Jess said.

"Yeah, that's true," Eddie agreed. In all the mayhem, he had yet to process that Christmas morning was only a few hours away. "All the more reason for us to hustle to that access tunnel."

Jess rested her hand on both of their shoulders. "We go direct and fast. You ready, Trinity?"

"It's now or never if we want out of this shit show."

Eddie set off at a brisk pace, carefully picking his way through the edge of the forest. Once his boots made contact with the snow-covered cobblestones, he broke into a fast jog. The other two kept up, weapons raised.

He peered into a few of the brightly lit stores. They appeared even more antiquated in the artificial light. The bakery had old cake stands inside a glass counter. When he passed the door, the scent of baking gingerbread invaded his nostrils. This had always been a comforting smell, like pencil shavings or cut grass, but his world had been turned upside down.

Next door, the restaurant-diner had ancient-looking booths inside and a faded menu plastered in the window. For a split second, he thought he detected movement inside, but it was just a chef's hat on the counter, casting a long shadow across the cramped dining area.

Every place had tacky Christmas decorations, mostly tinsel and balls, hanging off the display items.

The sheer effort to create this bewildering hunting ground was not lost on him. It must have taken thousands of hours and meticulous planning over the course of years.

And one thing was very apparent—the remaining survivors faced a focused, driven enemy with great inventiveness and a hunger for murder.

A gust of wind moaned along the street, showering everyone with flakes.

Nobody slowed their stride.

The group's boots and shoes crushed the snow as they advanced.

It took a lung-busting minute to reach the town square.

The music played even louder in this part of Old Forge. The song came to an end, then started again.

Eddie headed to the right side of the Christmas tree. The newsstand stood in darkness, made visible only by the light seeping out of the cracks of its closed hatch. He rounded it and came across a simple door on the far side. Jess skidded to a stop by his side. Shortly afterward, Trinity staggered around the corner. They all took a moment to catch their breath.

Jess lowered the door handle, pushed, but it didn't budge.

"No time for being subtle," Eddie said.

He lunged forward, hammering his shoulder against the flimsy-looking door. It buckled, but held.

Eddie battered the door three more times.

Again, it stayed in place.

However, the newsstand itself groaned and seemed to be leaning about a yard across the cobblestones.

"Gimme a hand to push," Eddie ordered.

The three of them shoved with all their might, and inch by inch, the stand moved toward the Christmas tree.

Finally, a grate appeared underneath the newsstand. It was circular, with thick steel bars. Easily enough space to fit through once they lifted it.

Beneath the grate, three recessed lights brightened the walls of a shaft. As in the bunker shaft, a ladder had been bolted to the concrete, leading down to the mouth of a tunnel below. Once the group had pushed the newsstand clear, they took a closer look, their breaths fogging and joining in the bitter night air.

For a moment, it had all seemed too easy. Then images of Tank's disintegrating neck, Greg's torn-out guts, and Damien Hurst's squashed face raced through Eddie's mind in a visceral and unspeakable way.

Crucially, though, nobody had approached and the square remained empty. Plus, the hatch was clearly designed to be hidden away from prying eyes. They still had time to escape. The only detectable presence was the warped Christmas song coming through the speakers, repeating endlessly on loop.

"Here goes nothing . . ." Eddie dropped to a crouch, wrapped his hands around two of the metal bars, and heaved the grate upward.

24

The steel bars weighed a ton. Eddie gritted his teeth, wrenching it with everything he had. It eventually came loose with a metallic grind, and he forced it up a few more inches. Jess grabbed the edge and helped flip over the heavy grate.

The rapid journey through the forest, moving the newsstand, and freeing the grate had kept the freezing conditions at the back of Eddie's mind. The rush from finding the access tunnel had also given him a burst of energy.

"Want me to head down?" he asked.

"Actually, I think I'm next in rotation," Trinity said. "Guess it's my turn to go first."

Eddie smiled. "I'm impressed by your courage."

"What? If there's a psycho down there, I'll fuck him up."

The three glanced at each other with serious looks, then broke into grins. Maybe it was relief at finding a way out. Or perhaps dark humor in the face of adversity. Or just a release of stress. Whatever the case, for a few seconds, the three of them shared a quiet moment of camaraderie.

"Go for it, Trinity," Jess encouraged.

Trinity dropped to the snow and crawled backward. Her legs disappeared into the tunnel and thudded against the ladder rungs. She lowered herself a few feet, grabbing the side rails, until only her head was exposed aboveground.

"Nice and easy," Eddie said.

"That's usually my way."

"Be careful. Shout if you see anything."

She smiled back at him. "You'll hear me scream."

Trinity climbed down another few steps to the sound of the same repeated holiday song booming through a distant speaker.

Eddie and Jess stepped to the mouth of the shaft to watch her descend. He quickly scanned in all directions, but it seemed that still, nobody was wise to their plan—against the odds, the group's luck had held. The hint of optimism in his mind had started to flourish.

Trinity descended another step, hands still raised high on the rail.

She lowered her left leg.

Suddenly, a laser beam speared out of the wall and created a small red dot on her ankle. It appeared her leg had triggered a sensor. Eddie opened his mouth to shout a warning.

Before any words could come out, another razor-sharp grate zipped across the shaft, slicing off all eight of Trinity's fingers, save her thumbs. It slammed across the shaft into a closed position, though Eddie could still see through the gaps.

Trinity let out a piercing scream as she plunged downward toward the access tunnel floor. Her back slammed hard against the concrete, and her head whipped back and struck the ground, sending her eyes into a spin.

Blood spurted from her eight severed digits. She tried to scream again, but the fall had knocked the wind out of her.

To her left, metal bars thrust down, blocking the tunnel entrance. She was trapped in a cage, twenty feet below the street.

A loud clank echoed up the shaft.

She had no way out.

And her severed fingers sat on top of the grate.

J ess looked across to Eddie. He couldn't get out any words about the sudden turn of events. She dropped to her knees and peered down at Trinity.

"Trinity, are you okay?!" Jess yelled. "Wake up. Focus."

Slowly, Trinity shook off the daze, and stared in horror at her blood-soaked hands. She screamed again, long, loud, and gurgling.

"Stay calm!" Jess shouted down. "We're gonna get you out!"

"Help," she whimpered back, sobbing uncontrollably.

Halfway down the shaft, a metal rod extended out of the wall at a steady speed. It had a digital thermometer attached, with a temperature reading of 0 degrees. Even colder than Jess had estimated after they'd left the forest hideout.

Trinity shivered and writhed below, lying in a pool of her own blood.

Jess went to grab the grate but quickly retracted her hand. The bars had sharp, glinting edges at each side. Impossible to hold with any force. She whipped her boot down, but the sturdy metal didn't move a millimeter.

"It slid into the opposite side of the wall," Eddie said desperately. "We'll never move it."

"We have to try!" Jess looked back down at Trinity. "Stay with us, girl. We'll find something to pry open the grate."

Trinity didn't respond. She stared down at her stumps, wide-eyed, lips trembling, legs rigid. Everything about her situation screamed death. But they couldn't simply give up on her.

Jess grabbed Eddie's shoulder. "See if you can find anything in the newsstand."

He quickly turned and headed to the wooden structure.

"Please . . . help me," Trinity moaned.

Jess lunged back to the top of the shaft.

A couple of yards above Trinity, three nozzles appeared from the sides of the wall, whirring mechanically.

"What's happening, Jess?" she screamed.

"I don't know."

Ice-cold water roared from each nozzle, aiming directly down onto Trinity, spraying her, drenching her clothes and face.

She shook from the sudden dousing.

"Get on your feet," Jess bellowed.

"I can't. I can't," she cried.

"You'll freeze—"

Two sections of the wall in front of and behind Trinity dropped into the floor, revealing two industrial-strength box fans. Both were protected by the same bars that had blocked the way to the tunnel. Their motors simultaneously hummed to life, and the blades rapidly spun to a blur.

"What the hell?!" Jess shouted. "Try to get out of the wind!"

Trinity, face scrunched in agony, managed to move into a sitting position. The fans blasted against her soaking-wet body.

The temperature reading in the shaft had already dropped to 5 degrees below zero.

Eddie staggered back from the newsstand, holding a short steel pole and a plank of wood. He dropped them by the mouth of the shaft and let out a gasp. "What the fuck?"

"It's a trap," Jess told him. "We need to get her out, right now."

The nozzles of frigid water sprayed Trinity again, soaking her further.

Then, the box fans roared back to life.

Minus 10.

Trinity screamed until her lungs emptied.

Eddie wedged the pipe into a gap in the grate. He slammed

his foot down on the raised piece of metal, but it didn't budge. He stomped down again and again, cursing with each strike.

Jess grabbed his arm. "It's not working!"

At the bottom of the shaft, Trinity had crossed her arms, her injured hands having started to freeze, leaving strings of sticky blood dangling from the stumps. Ice crystals had begun to form on her coat and hair. She shivered uncontrollably as the temperature dipped even further.

Jess looked at the temperature gauge in the shaft.

Minus 15.

"Stay with us!" Jess shouted. She turned to Eddie. "We need more leverage. Use the plank."

"It isn't stronger than steel."

"Just try it, dammit!"

They jammed the plank into the grate. Gripped the other end of the six-foot length and shoved it down. The wood splintered and cracked. Once again, though, the grate refused to budge.

Jess cleared away the broken timber.

Eddie tried with the pipe again, but it was no use. Every second they fought a futile battle against the well-constructed barrier brought Trinity closer and closer to her end.

Below, the water sprayed again, followed by the whirring of the industrial fans.

Minus 20.

More ice had formed on Trinity's clothing, exposing raw skin. Her hair suddenly had a salt-and-pepper appearance. Her breathing had become shallow and rapid, forming small clouds in front of her parted lips.

Eddie rammed his boot against the grate several times.

"Trinity!" Jess shouted. "Look up!"

She didn't react.

"Look up. Stay with us!"

Slowly, Trinity raised her head, but the movement threw her stiff body off balance. She toppled backward into the freezing water.

Trinity lay there, arms still crossed, though her shaking had almost ceased. She stared straight up, stony-faced.

"Trinity!" Eddie roared.

The water sprayed her again, followed by the fans whirring to life.

Minus 25.

A thick sheet of ice had hardened around Trinity's face and body.

Jess wrapped an arm around Eddie. It was obvious what was coming next, and the act of comforting him gave her comfort too.

Trinity stopped breathing for a few seconds.

"Trinity!" Eddie shouted again. "GET UP!"

Jess gazed down, waiting for any sign of movement. Any sign of life.

She knew there was no way of getting through the gate in time to save her, and that even if they could, in this condition she was already too far gone.

Trinity's body resembled an ice sculpture carved out of a single block with an axe, frozen in time forever.

A final breath emerged from Trinity's lips, creating a small patch of mist above her face. The box fans unceremoniously blew it away. Her face still looked directly up the shaft, but at that moment, the light left her eyes.

Jess bowed her head and shuddered.

Trinity was gone.

25

He slunk back into the shadows of the nearby town hall doorway to avoid detection. His breathing had become erratic after experiencing the thrill of the hunt once more. It was clear the woman called Trinity had died in that tunnel below. The two other survivors stood above the concealed passage, distraught looks on their faces.

The man licked his lips. More than anything, he wanted to take a look at the work up close. To witness the magnificence of a creation that had just snared another unwitting victim. This town *dripped* with his kind of poetry.

And best of all, despite the sound of the same annoying song coming through the town's speakers, he was close enough to the two remaining survivors to hear every word of their desperate conversation. To watch their body language, riddled with despair.

"My God, Eddie," the woman said, whimpering. With that, she rose and buried her head in his chest.

He embraced her, and the two held each other for a moment.

"I know, Jess," the man replied.

Eddie and Jess.

He wondered if they'd been intimate yet. Moments like this, when one was faced with impending death, human behavior changed. Perhaps it was a mixture of fear and lust, the adrenaline of the moment, the meaninglessness of life in the face of mortality. He knew that in moments like this, primal instincts came to the fore. He could attest to that.

It was a shame that their blossoming relationship would end soon. But it was them or him. No other equation existed in his mind.

The distant pair separated a moment later and continued their conversation. "What do we do now?" Jess asked.

"The entire place is a trap. I don't see much of a choice. We head back to the bunker, barricade ourselves in, and wait until morning. We'll face tomorrow at the gates when it comes."

The woman nodded in agreement. "At least we'll face it together."

She squeezed his hand tenderly.

Watching the display of affection, even from a distance, was sickening.

These two deserve to die.

The two strangers turned to head back toward the bunker. The last thing he heard Eddie say was, "We can keep an eye on the cameras in the control room, try to spot the asshole who is still out here . . ."

"Asshole"?

That was disrespectful toward a man who had outsmarted them. Who had closely followed their every move without a hint of detection. He didn't care, though. He'd expected this kind of stupidity. Their brain-dead attitudes would see them go the same way as the others. He'd celebrate Christmas as the last man standing. The sole winner of a competition that he was built to win.

I'm a machine.

And he knew the location of every single camera in this town. And how to avoid them at his leisure.

Eddie and Jess made their way along the main street, trudging past the brightly lit stores. Once they had disappeared from view, he stepped out of the doorway.

His excitement grew as he neared Trinity.

This wasn't just a death scene. It was a smartly crafted tableau. An homage to the secret world he lived in. A tip of the hat to a reality that fools in their comfort zones would deny even existed. The true nature of man.

He picked up one of the dead woman's severed fingers. Held it close to his face, marveling at the immaculately precise cut that had carved through flesh and bone. He put the finger in his pocket as a piece for his private trophy collection. Then he stepped toward an even better sight.

The man stared down in awe at Trinity's corpse. She was frozen in time and space, her head looking straight up toward a salvation that would never come. An ever-thickening shell of ice covered her entire body. Sprays of water and the whirring of fans continued to blast her corpse.

The scene was literally perfect. It was like peering into a snow globe at a masterfully crafted piece of art suspended inside.

It was a shame he hadn't seen the moment of her death. That pleasure had been reserved for Jess and Eddie.

The thought of those two broke him from his reverie.

By now, they would have made it back into the forest.

He headed back to the main street. Stayed close to the buildings on the left side of the road. Kept under the awnings. Out of camera shot. Moved at a steady pace, tracking the freshest footprints in the snow.

Once in the forest, he had to tread more carefully.

The lights from the town cast long shadows between the

trees. He darted from trunk to trunk, stealthily. The type of tactical movement that was way beyond Jess and Eddie's skill set.

They would only be a minute or two ahead, clumsily searching for the subterranean entrance that they had camouflaged before leaving. He'd been inside the underground control center after they'd headed back to town, but only for a minute. He didn't understand why they had left the safety of the bunker.

The reasoning didn't matter, but it had cost Trinity her life.

He passed the corpse with the crushed face. This person was no more than a grisly prop. His body had been here since the start, undoubtedly to strike the fear of God into the group upon discovery.

Another few minutes of weaving between the trees brought him close enough to hear voices ahead.

These two . . . *Eddie and Jess* . . . had no idea they were being followed.

Good for him.

Deadly for them.

And he would enjoy every minute of their demise, starting with Eddie.

Jess will take me a bit more time . . .

Jess stopped as soon as the silhouette of the concrete bunker appeared through the darkness. She motioned Eddie behind the closest tree. They stood there in silence, waiting, watching, and listening. The faint Christmas music from town drifted on the breeze. The same song again, with the same thinly veiled warning.

For a second, she thought she heard someone following.

A breaking branch, pine needles being crushed, or a kicked stone colliding with a rock. Something sounded in the forest.

She placed her finger to her lips and pointed back in the direction of the town.

Eddie visually searched in that direction.

But no more suspicious noises were heard over the next few minutes. It could have been her paranoia, or the memory of the grizzly bear ripping Greg to pieces . . .

And the cold had started to chill Jess to the bone again. Tonight was far colder than last night, and with sunset near, she guessed the temperature would continue to plummet.

"Let's go for it," she whispered.

"You think anyone's inside?"

"Maybe. But it'll be two against one."

Eddie leaned toward her. "What makes you think this is one guy?"

"It takes a special kind of person to kill people in this way."

Jess rounded the tree and advanced to where the frozen cable lay on the ground. She followed it to where the group had scattered branches over the latch door. Eddie and she kicked them to the side.

He heaved open the wooden entrance.

She climbed down, grimacing as her hands gripped the ladder's freezing rails. For a second, she imagined Trinity's final descent into that access tunnel a few minutes earlier. The look of optimism on her face before the second grate sliced her fingers off.

The terrifying look in her eyes as she froze to death. The final, meaningless last breath she took.

It was all so clinical.

Jess's boots thudded against the concrete at the entrance to the bunker. She spun the hatch and had it open by the time Eddie reached her side.

They entered the first room's welcoming warmth, weapons raised.

Eddie stormed straight to the control room. A short time later, he returned. "We're alone. Let's secure the place."

They shut the wheel lock and pushed three of the filing cabinets behind the door.

To Jess, this was the safest space inside the electrified perimeter. It had heat, supplies, and visibility of the town. The perfect place to shelter until Christmas morning.

They went through to the control room and sat on the two swivel chairs.

Eddie peered at each of the monitors in turn.

Jess had guessed earlier yesterday that he was the strongest in the group, and her guess had been correct.

He spun around in his chair and caught her eye.

"What are you looking at?" he asked.

"Yesterday in the chapel, if someone would have told me only two of us would be left alive by tonight, and they forced me to guess who, I probably would've picked you as one of them."

He smiled at her. "I would have picked you too."

26

Eddie allowed himself a brief moment of relaxation. The underground hideout was relatively secure, he had begun to defrost, and the chances of seeing Christmas morning had grown in his mind.

Jess melted into her chair, her body and mind exhausted, confirmed by the dark rings around her eyes. But she still had that quiet authority about her that Eddie had grown to like more and more.

That was only one consideration, though. He wondered just how much of an emotional impact the horrendous events of the past two days would have on both of them—if they pulled through.

Seeing what we've seen . . .

His stomach growled, and he swallowed to moisten his throat. This was the first time he had allowed himself to take stock of his personal situation. No food or sleep for twenty-four hours. The best thing he'd had to eat was melted snow off a collection plate. The worst thing of all was the relentless anxiety of being pursued by an invisible and uncompromising enemy.

Eddie gazed toward the kitchenette.

"Are you starving?" Jess asked. "I know I am."

"Do you wanna risk anything from the fridge?"

She pursed her lips. "I might."

"Really?"

"I don't think this place was meant to be discovered by us.

Look around—the monitors, the innermost secrets of this town, this hunt. This bunker wasn't created with us in mind. There's a better-than-average chance the food is fine."

"Okay, you be the royal taster."

She gave him a tired nod. "I'm not that desperate yet."

He returned his focus to the video feeds. Once again, the entire town appeared deserted. He kept the closest eye on the screens that displayed the area around the hideout's hatch, the electrified gates that led to the farmhouse, and the shaft that led down to the access tunnel. They seemed the most likely areas for someone to appear.

"Mind if I ask you a question?" Jess said.

"Sure."

"I noticed that you never said why you are here."

"You're right, I didn't," Eddie replied, still monitoring the screens. "I suppose out of guilt, or embarrassment, or distrust."

"I'd say we're past that at this point."

"True." He spun his chair to face Jess. "Plus, my entire life history is right there, in that file. So I suppose there's no reason for secrecy anymore. Take a look if you want."

"I'd kinda rather hear it directly from you, know what I mean? Understand how you got here."

He nodded, knowing what she meant. There was nothing to lose anymore by telling his tale of woe. In another world, at another time, he'd offer to buy her a drink.

"You remember I said the old couple injected me with something in the grocery store's parking lot?"

"Yes. Go on."

"Well, I left out one important detail. I tried to rob them first."

She gave him a reprimanding look. "Eddie."

"I know. I'm not proud of it. She flashed a couple of thousand dollars in her purse. I didn't think they'd miss it. Not that that's an excuse." He let out a deep sigh. "So there you are. I've been stealing shit for as long as I can remember. When I was younger, I rolled with a harder crowd, did some armed robberies, some home invasions. One that . . ."

Eddie drifted away into the recesses of his memory, regret pouring over his face.

Jess waited patiently for the rest, and Eddie snapped out of it a moment later.

He cleared his throat and continued. "But the past few years, it became more just crimes of opportunity, you know? I'm trying. This was gonna be the last, it really was."

"But this time, I'm guessing you chose the wrong target."

"See, that's the thing. Their file on me is years in the making. There's a picture of my car outside a local bar in Fort Drum. I haven't been there in months. They've been tracking me for a while now."

"I thought the same thing about Greg after hearing his story."

"Another thing, though. Take a look at our group. Our variety of crimes is way too broad. I doubt this is personal, at all."

"I think that's a fair assumption," Jess said. "We were all targeted for different reasons. You and I are nothing like Trinity."

"Right."

It made sense in his mind, though it made the situation even more chilling. Their captors had been scouting criminals—some who had even evaded authorities—to hand out their own form of fucked-up justice.

Tank and his drugs. Greg and his fraud. Trinity and her hit-and-run. Him and his light fingers. And . . .

Eddie leaned forward in his chair. "Why are you here, Jess?"

Jess stared at him for a moment, piercing and direct. He felt she was sizing him up, debating whether she could trust him or not.

She sighed. "Addiction."

"Addiction? Really? You don't seem the type."

"Yeah, well, we come in all shapes and sizes, I suppose. I've struggled with containing it for as long as I can remember."

He recognized a deep sorrow in her eyes. The type he had witnessed in his father's eyes after his mother had died from a brain hemorrhage. The despair of knowing how futile our efforts are in life.

"There's been good years and bad," she said. "My parents bore the brunt of it when I was younger, first with denial, then with trying to punish me for it. I remember when I was a teenager, they locked me in my room for extended periods of time, trying to get me to quit. And I did . . . for a while. Tried to live a normal life, had a boyfriend, graduated college. I was one hell of an architect, too, for a time. But it *always* came back. Addiction destroys everything and everyone it touches, know what I mean?"

Eddie nodded.

"Eventually, after a very long time, my parents accepted it. I really didn't give them any other choice."

"So you're still hooked?"

Jess's eyes glazed over as she looked past Eddie, as if she were searching out there somewhere in the far corner of the room for the answer. "You never beat addiction, Eddie. You can go a certain amount of time without getting a fix, but it's always there in the background, lurking, gnawing at your mind, begging you to take a hit. I can feel it right now. The urge, coursing through every part of me. It's in my bones. I used to try to convince myself this will be the last one. But it never is. It's never, ever enough."

Jess locked eyes with him. "So now, I don't fight it anymore. It's who I am. This'll be with me for the rest of my life."

He rested a hand on her shoulder. "Heroin, meth, coke, whatever. You're a good person, Jess. I know you'll beat it in the end."

"You're not understanding me, Eddie. *I don't want to beat it.*"

The sudden intensity of her gaze made Eddie uneasy. He averted his eyes, turning them back toward the screens to scan for anyone approaching. All was quiet on the monitors.

"I'm sorry," Jess said. "I made you uncomfortable. I shared too much."

"No, it's okay, really." He returned his eyes to her. "I appreciate you being so honest with me. Everyone always bitches about how they want to change, including me. It's just unusual to hear someone say 'Fuck it, this is who I am.' Know what I mean?"

"Well then. Fuck it. This is who I am."

Eddie smiled at her. "Right on."

"Screw this," Jess said eventually. "I'm going for it."

She rose from her chair and headed to the kitchenette. Less than a minute later, she returned with two bottles of water, a sealed packet of cookies, and two apples. She placed them on the table in front of a small couch.

He gave her a wary look and sat next to her on the couch. "You really wanna risk it?"

Jess unscrewed the cap from a bottle of water. She poured out a small amount and dipped the end of her index finger in it. She bent down and sniffed the liquid.

"Seems okay to me," she said.

"Could be drugged."

"Or it could just be water."

Jess took a sip, washed it around her mouth, and swallowed. She stared at Eddie.

"So?" he asked.

"Not bad—"

Jess clutched her throat with both hands. She let out a long, pained wheeze. Her wide eyes locked with Eddie's in fear.

He bolted from the sofa. "Jess! What the hell! I told you—"

Her body relaxed and straightened. A broad grin stretched across her face.

"You jackass!" he spat.

"Sorry. Couldn't resist."

Jess took a few more chugs of water. She unscrewed the other bottle, took a mouthful, and handed it to Eddie. "This one's fine too."

He took a small sip. Held the water in his mouth for a few moments before swallowing. Nothing bad happened.

Eddie took four large gulps.

Next, they tried the apples. Once again, they seemed good as he greedily chomped on the tough skin and bittersweet insides. A piece of fruit had never tasted so good. And the water had already started to make him feel more alive.

They grabbed a few cookies each and sank into the couch cushions, their bodies truly unwinding for the first time in days. Eddie rested his feet on the table and stared at the screen showing Old Forge's main street.

For a second, his vision blurred.

Eddie yawned.

The comfort, warmth, and food had brought forward his

own exhaustion. He guessed it was from the adrenaline finally waning in his body.

He glanced over at Jess, who was also struggling to stay awake. She closed her eyes, and leaned against Eddie's shoulder on the comfortable couch.

He was surprised by the natural intimacy of the moment, and welcomed it. He watched her drift off, while fighting his own drooping eyelids.

But before he surrendered to the sweet embrace of sleep, a pang of guilt rose up in his chest. Guilt for lying to Jessica a few moments ago, when confessing their innermost secrets to each other.

He left something out. Something that he'd never forgive himself for . . .

Fifteen years earlier

The sound of chirping crickets filled the humid summer air. Eddie followed his buddy Marco through a thin stretch of forest toward the northern bank of Lake Oneida. Moonlight guided them toward their target, and the promise of a large score.

"How much further?" Eddie whispered.

"Shut up. We're nearly there."

Sweat had soaked his T-shirt despite its being only a half-mile hike from their parked car. Driving directly up to the secluded house would have taken them past multiple security cameras, and better to be safe than sorry. Nobody had seen them so far. And he felt sure the coast would be clear when they left.

Marco threw his arm across Eddie's chest as they neared the lake house's long, neatly manicured backyard. They crouched in silence, staring toward the property of the retired Fort Drum physician, Dr. Franks.

The two-story Colonial, painted in striking white with an ornate veranda, screamed money. Something about it also screamed danger.

"There are lights on inside," Eddie said. "You said he wasn't home."

Marco let out a long, deep breath. "He isn't. I've scoped out the place for two full days. Old man skipped town, probably taking synchronized swimming lessons in Boca Raton or some shit that rich people do. I don't fucking know."

"So why the lights?"

"Jeez, your bro said you were impressionable, not stupid. They're on a timer, dumbass."

"You're sure?"

Marco edged closer, eyes narrowed. "Yeah man, I'm sure. You wanna keep stealing twenties from people's pockets, go right ahead. Or you wanna grow some goddamn balls for a change. Decide now, Eddie."

A look of resolve spread across Eddie's face. "Okay, let's do it."

"You'll be thanking me soon, bro."

Eddie followed Marco as they jogged to the backyard. They hugged the left edge of the lawn, staying in the shadows of the trees.

Dead bugs and leaves floated on the surface of the in-ground pool, suggesting it hadn't been used for days. Dr. Franks's recognizable Plymouth Barracuda was not in the driveway. Those two facts helped boost Eddie's confidence. This was a big step up from raiding a rickety shack for booze and porn.

Marco picked up his pace toward the back door.

This was the first time Eddie had worked with him. The fast-talking, opportunistic criminal was his brother's buddy. They had met at a barbecue last month, and their conversation had led them here. Despite Eddie's reluctance, Marco had sold the idea, with the help of a few shots of tequila.

Empty house, in and out. They'd make more money in a half hour than Eddie had made in the past year. The idea was too tempting to let pass.

The old widower, Franks, had been known in Fort Drum for his flamboyancy and his taste for the finer things in life. It was totally conceivable that there'd be rich pickings here.

Marco peered through a few of the windows.

Eddie stepped close behind, checking out the dimly lit kitchen and a retro dining room. Nothing stirred in the lake house and nothing moved outside. At one in the morning, he guessed most people in the surrounding properties were tucked up in bed or out of town on summer vacation.

"Down there," Marco said, pointing at a blacked-out basement window. "That's the room we've got to get into."

Apparently, a contact had told Marco that Dr. Franks's lower level was a treasure trove of shit.

They approached the back door of the house.

Eddie wanted to show some nerve. Prove he wasn't just a passenger in this venture. He lowered the handle and pushed, but it was locked.

"Do you know how to pick—"

Without hesitation, Marco shattered the thin glass with his elbow, making a sound too loud for Eddie's liking.

Marco thrust his hand through, turned the latch, and opened the door.

"See?" he said. "Like candy from a baby."

They entered the quiet house.

The moonlight cast long shadows through the large living area. Out of the front windows, Lake Oneida glistened, a few anchored pleasure boats gently bobbing on its surface. For a moment, Eddie dreamed of living this life. Money and comfort. Far away from his temptations.

"This way," Marco said. "Let's do it fast."

He pushed Eddie toward the basement entrance.

Each step down induced a creak from the wooden staircase that echoed through the spacious house. The air in the house seemed thick enough to scoop, and sweat quickly poured down Eddie's face. There was no air-conditioning on in the house, further increasing Eddie's confidence in their venture.

Eddie slowed as he reached the final few steps because of a light being on in one of the basement rooms, but Marco shoved him forward.

Eddie staggered into the basement.

And came face-to-face with a wheelchair-ridden, wide-eyed Doctor Franks.

The old man was sitting by a record player surrounded by Sinatra memorabilia. He held an unlit cigar a few inches from his lips and a Zippo in his other hand. An open bottle of Fernet-Branca sat nearby.

Eddie and the man stared at each other for a few seconds.

A fleeting look of recognition crossed the physician's face. Maybe he'd recalled that years ago he'd given Eddie his shots as a kid, or tried to put his dad on a better path. Regardless, the sight of Franks, now a scared, withered shadow of the jovial man who used to care for his family, made Eddie instantly stop.

Marco barged past him, pistol raised. "Listen up, old man. Stay cool and we'll be gone before you know it. You got me?"

"T-t-take what you want," Franks stuttered. "Just leave me alone."

Eddie wanted to tell Marco to put the gun down.

But he resisted the urge.

Maybe that's how these things go down.

I'm being naïve.

Pictures of Franks and his family adorned the walls. With his wife and two daughters on a cruise. At a pool party, singing into a microphone. On a family vacation in Antigua. Franks clearly inebriated at Epcot. A framed portrait of the Rat Pack in the center of the wall. A medal for saving a man's life at a highway rest stop. All the trappings of a well-lived, honorable life.

Eddie glanced across to his partner for a lead on their next move.

Marco seemed completely at ease. Cool and calculating. He strode over to a locked oak cabinet, gun still pointed at the doctor, and said, "Is this where you keep your shit?"

"Here, I've got money," Franks replied. He dug his hand into his trouser pocket and pulled out a wallet. "There's about four hundred dollars in there."

"Fuck your cash, old man. I want more than that."

Marco used the handle of his gun to slam the cabinet lock downward. The door opened with relative ease. He opened the various drawers inside the cabinet in rapid succession.

"Jackpot."

Eddie leaned over to look at the contents of the cabinet. There were decades of jewelry inside, no doubt all real. Gold necklaces, brooches, even a tennis bracelet that had to be worth ten grand or more. And in the center, a spectacular wedding ring with more diamonds in it than Eddie had seen in his entire life.

"Please," Franks pleaded, "not my wife's jewelry. I'm begging you."

"Don't think she needs it no more, bro," Marco said callously.

He slipped off his backpack, knelt, and opened it.

Eddie stood motionless while Marco dumped handfuls of gold and silver into the bag. A creeping sense of guilt had crept over him. If Franks wasn't here, sure, he would have felt differently. This, though. Seeing the fear and anger on the old man's face. He tried not to make eye contact with him.

A metallic squeak broke him from his thoughts. Dr. Franks moved closer to Eddie.

"I know you."

Eddie turned away from the doctor, as if that would shield his identity.

"I do," Dr. Franks continued. "You're Billy's boy."

"Shut the hell up, old man," Marco yelled, while still emptying the contents of the drawers into his backpack.

"It's Eddie, right?" the old man asked. "I remember your mom too. I was there with her when she passed."

Eddie faced away from the doctor, embarrassed by his behavior. This had all been a mistake.

"I said shut the fuck up!" Marco shouted.

The old man wheeled closer to Eddie, his voice softening.

"Listen, son. You don't need to do this, either of you. We can just forget about it all. It's not too late to change this."

Marco quickened his pace, indiscriminately throwing shit into his bag as fast as possible.

Eddie remained turned away from the old man. Tears welled up in his eyes. Franks was there when his mom died. Eddie was out making a score, and didn't learn of his mother's death till hours later. He'd never forget the look on his father's face that day. The anguish, the disappointment in his son.

The old man wheeled closer still.

"Look at me, Eddie. You at least owe me the courtesy of looking me in my eyes."

Eddie shook his head no, his face still turned away from the doctor.

"I said look at me, son."

"That's all of it!" Marco yelled. "Let's go!" He sprinted toward the staircase.

Eddie whipped around to follow suit, but didn't realize how closely the old man had maneuvered behind him. He crashed into the man's wheelchair full force, sending it tipping backward.

Eddie desperately attempted to grab the bars of the wheelchair, but they slipped out of his reach.

The old man flipped backward and crashed hard into the basement floor. When his frail body came to an abrupt stop, his head whipped back and cracked against the unforgiving concrete.

Marco stopped on the staircase and looked back at the scene.

Eddie knelt on the floor beside Dr. Franks. The old man's eyes bulged, and his head lay still.

Eddie cupped the back of the man's head to see if he was all right. He felt an odd, wet sensation in his palms. When he pulled his hands away, they were covered in blood.

A pool of thick maroon liquid spread out from under the doctor's scalp, his face frozen and contorted in pain.

"No, no, no . . ." Eddie scrambled away from the body, taking in sharp breaths of air. He got to his feet and backed away, slamming into the cabinet.

He looked down at his hands, dripping with the doctor's blood.

He did this.

He killed him.

Marco shouted from the railing.

Let's fucking go, Eddie!

C'mon, let's go!

Let's go!

Eddie could still hear the echo of Marco's angry voice screaming at him from the staircase all those years ago.

How had his life led him to that?

How could he live with himself?

He shook off the memory, pushed the guilt to the back of his mind, and closed his eyes.

Eddie's chin sagged on his chest, and he began to drift off to sleep against Jessica, praying that if he had a dream, it would be about something better than all this.

27

The man crept through the pitch-black forest, barely containing his excitement. He considered himself the apex predator in this domain, remaining undiscovered in the wilderness, avoiding detection like a pro.

Tonight, an icy wind brushed through the forest. Not that it mattered. Any climate or culture suited him well. He was a global chameleon, but a local's nightmare. He was too primed for the vast majority of humanity.

Snow blasted through the forest.

It induced a shiver.

He found the current weather invigorating. Pain was pleasure. Snow fell between the trees, evoking memories of his youth. Back in the day, he would stalk animals in the forest behind his house in Montana. Follow their prints with his old Cooey Model 64 rifle and hunting knife.

His biggest success had been a gray fox when he was eleven years old. An accurate shot had slowed it to a crawl, allowing him to walk alongside the animal, watching and waiting. Then, as a curious young man with a thirst for knowledge, he'd carried out an autopsy on the fox, executing precision cuts to inspect the organs. He ripped out a few teeth to create a necklace trophy. He tried to make a hat out of its pelt, though that didn't work.

But he had graduated from animals a long time ago.

They had been his training to meet his real desires.

He peered up at a security camera that had been surreptitiously strapped to a pine tree. It angled down on the concrete building's front door. The man had considered putting it out of commission, but that would have probably alerted Eddie and Jess to his presence nearby.

Instead, he stayed out of camera range and headed around the back of the concrete building to consider his next move. He leaned against the cold cinder block wall, imagining the deaths of the two useless creatures that had descended underground in the nearby bunker.

Like rats.

Vermin.

Would they fall into another trap? There were no guarantees in this town. He considered if he'd have to do the dirty work himself. Precision swings with his axe. Lethal blows to the head and body. It would require only his masterful technique, and very little effort.

Eddie first.

He wanted time alone with Jess before putting her out of her misery.

The man kicked around the torn newspaper clippings on the ground outside the building.

His mind raced with visions of Trinity, frozen like a statue.

He swallowed hard and let out a shuddering breath.

Observing the aftermath of the deaths was no longer satisfying his needs. The gruesome death scenes had only served to stoke his inner beast. Once it was stirred up, he knew the beast needed feeding.

It was playtime. His way. Uncompromising and hard.

The man ran his finger along the axe's blade.

The sharpness sliced open his skin.

He licked the wound. The warm, coppery blood filled his mouth. It was a ritual he had observed many times. And it meant only one thing would happen in the next few minutes.

There was no going back.

His time was now.

He stepped out from behind the bunker and followed the length of exposed cable that led twenty yards away to the hidden underground bunker. No matter what barricades they constructed inside, it would take an army to hold him back. He'd come at them so fast that they wouldn't know what hit them.

The weight of the axe felt good—

A bright spark flashed to his left, catching his eye.

Something zipped through the misty air.

Two barbs bit into the side of his chest.

Tremendous amounts of electricity suddenly surged through his body.

By the time he realized he'd been Tasered, he'd collapsed.

The man couldn't move. His brain shook like a peanut in a jar. It felt like wasps were crawling through his veins. He tried to shout, but only a string of drool came out of his mouth.

His mind swirled with confusion. He tried to collect his thoughts, to think of a way out. How could this have happened?

A dark figure slowly appeared over his body.

The figure slipped a noose around his neck, walked behind him, and yanked hard.

As pain continued to rush through his body, he blacked out.

He came to with a splitting headache. His eyes slammed open, and he looked up at the trees and dark clouds. The cold, damp ground had penetrated the back of his clothing. His body trembled and his teeth chattered.

Have I been left here?

Did some idiot try to teach me a lesson?

Me?

Then he remembered the Tasering. He reached for his neck.

The noose ripped tightly against his throat in response. His body scraped a few inches along the ground.

The dark figure yanked at the noose again. He gasped for breath and tried to grab the rope with both hands.

The axe handle—now in the possession of his captor—rushed out of the darkness and battered against his fingers, sending pain searing through his arms.

The man's hands fell away instinctively from the blow.

"Who are you?" he cried out.

The figure stayed silent.

"Stop!" he pleaded. "We're the same!"

Suddenly, the axe handle smashed against his forehead.

Blood trickled down the side of his face. He attempted to raise an arm to protect himself. The handle cracked against the back of his head.

His world turned to blackness once again.

His head pounded and felt ready to explode. He woke face down in the snow, struggling for breath. Lights flashed in his peripheral vision. He groggily raised his head to see where he'd been taken.

This time, he had regained consciousness on the main street of Old Forge. A dazzling streetlight bore down on him. To his left, a Santa decoration flashed in the saloon window. Every piece of brightness increased the pain in his eyes.

The dark figure stood in front of him, rope in hand as if holding a dog leash.

"Wait!" he begged. "I can help you!"

Ignoring his pleas, the figure gave the rope a strong tug.

He scrambled to all fours to avoid his face being dragged through the snow. The humiliation of being walked like a dog made him clench his teeth in anger. Once free, he would have his payback. He would do what came most naturally to him, what he knew better than anyone. Bind this person and strip them naked, have his piece, and leave the scene as the conqueror.

The dark figure continued to drag him forward. He tried to scramble to his feet and reach the cover of a store's awning. But he lost his balance, and his shoulder collided with the cobblestone road.

The axe handle rose above him.

"You don't understand," he yelled. "I'm an ally!"

The dark figure stood staring down, rope in one hand, axe in the other. He searched for any signs of emotion in the eyes, but met only an intense glare. It was this type of audacity that triggered him.

"Who the fuck are you?" he demanded.

The axe handle whipped down, hammering against his kneecap.

He roared with agony. "I'll fucking kill you slowly."

His threat induced several blows to his arms, chest, and neck, and the final one crashed into his temple.

This time, he woke in a standing position, propped against a freezing steel pole. His legs had been chained to it and secured with a padlock. His attacker forced his arms behind his back.

Handcuffs crunched around his wrists. Tightened, and tightened again. The metal restraints squeezed his bones.

Searing pain throbbed through all parts of his body. The last time he'd blacked out, he figured, the dark figure must have continued hitting him for a good while longer, breaking a few of his bones.

He blinked to clear the stars from his vision. Ahead, holiday decorations lit up the main street. He stood wonderingly in the town square.

They secured me to the outside edge of the merry-go-round?

The man strained to see behind him.

The dark figure stood by the ride's center pole.

Moments later, cheery organ music pumped from crackling speakers.

The merry-go-round began slowly turning, picking up speed.

The dark figure jumped off the ride and watched him revolve at a faster and faster pace. Then the figure jogged back along the main street. The sheer arrogance of it blew his mind.

"Get the fuck back here!" he yelled.

It seemed obvious that the plan for him was to either freeze to death or be shamed in front of Eddie and Jess.

If he was being offered up to those two as an easy kill, that would fail, because neither of them had the guts. They would release him. He would kill them. And then he would take his revenge.

The ride wound up to full speed, and he spun round and round, strapped to the outer pole, facing the dizzying town.

He struggled against the cuffs and chain.

It was no use. Only another person could free him from this trap. For that, he needed Eddie and Jess. He growled at the thought of having to rely on others—the victims in this game. But there was little choice.

A mechanical buzz broke into his thoughts.

And something rose from the ground that struck him with terror.

He screamed as loud as he could.

Then screamed again for help.

Because if somebody didn't come soon, he would suffer an even worse death than any of his victims.

28

Eddie's head rolled to the side on the couch. A muffled voice came from somewhere in the room, like somebody shouting underwater. He wanted to open his eyes, but his body fought against his will. He'd never experienced tiredness like this before. It was as if he were floating inside a thick cloud of haze and confusion.

"Eddie!" Jess shouted close to his ear. She shook his shoulder. "Get up!"

The sternness in her voice snapped him out of his semiconscious state. He scrambled upright on the couch, startled and confused.

"What's going on?" he asked.

"You gotta see this."

Eddie hauled himself up and they headed back into the control room. He couldn't think straight. His head pounded. This seemed more than just exhaustion, but Jess's urgency pushed that thought to the back of his mind for the moment.

She pointed up at a central monitor. "Look."

He squinted, trying to focus. The merry-go-round spun in the central square. On the second revolution, he noticed someone strapped to the outermost support pole of the ride. A man, judging by his figure. On the third turn it became obvious that whoever it was had been secured to the ride against his will.

"Any idea who it is?" Eddie muttered.

"I have a feeling it's about to be another victim. Look in front of the ride."

Something had risen out of the ground, very close to the edge of the merry-go-round. It was too hard to tell exactly what it was because of the poor picture quality, but it looked like a sharp metal blade.

Eddie watched the blade closely as the man swung round and round the ride.

"Jesus Christ," he muttered to himself. "Is that . . . is that blade . . . rising?"

"Huh?"

"Look. Look closely, watch for a minute."

Sure enough, it appeared as if the blade was ever so slowly rising up, perhaps a quarter of an inch at a time, getting closer and closer to the man's dangling feet above as he swung by.

Soon, the blade would reach the heels of the man's feet.

And then, ever so slowly . . .

"We can save him," Jess said with authority.

"You're suggesting we go there right now?"

"Do you wanna watch him die from here?"

"No," Eddie admitted. "But it could be a trap to lure us out."

"Can you live with yourself if we don't try?"

Eddie's mind drifted back to that old man bleeding out on the concrete floor in front of him so many years ago.

No. I couldn't live with myself.

He beat back the selfishness and desire for self-preservation. "You're right. Let's go fast, but carefully."

"You might want this." Jess swept a carving knife off the console and handed it to him. "Found a couple of better weapons in the kitchenette."

Eddie nodded. "Good work. We'd better hurry. There's not much time."

They cleared the barricade, climbed the ladder, and crept into the freezing forest again. Jess led the way, sprinting between the trees toward the distant lights and sound of music. She was nimble and fast.

Eddie tried to follow, but it took him a moment to become steady on his feet. He threw out his arms toward a tree, grabbing it at the last second to avoid tumbling over. Next, he set off at a sprint, and wobbled to his left and right, slamming against a tree trunk. He wasn't in control, but he followed as best he could, countering the odd sensations.

Am I stoned?

I'm not in control of my body.

Something's wrong . . .

The subzero temperature and the wind's raw edge helped shake his extremities awake and force him out of his slumber. He gave chase after Jess, sprinting toward the town center before it was too late.

Jess slowed as she approached the start of the cobblestone road.

A man's faint screams rose above the repeating Christmas song and the organ music of the merry-go-round.

Eddie eventually caught up to Jess.

She nodded in the direction of the town. "Come on."

They sprinted down the main street.

Light snow continued to fall, drifting into the glare of the streetlights, resting on top of the awnings and the flickering decorations. It gave the replica of Old Forge a much friendlier feel than it deserved.

As they closed on the town square, Eddie focused on the merry-go-round.

The man's feet had been chained to the outside bar of the ride, and his hands had been secured behind his back. He caught sight of Eddie and Jess and yelled something that got lost in the surrounding music.

They took a few rapid steps toward the ride.

Eddie skidded to a stop a few yards short.

A small hatch had opened in the ground, less than a foot away from the outer edge of the ride.

A piston arm protruded from the dark space, a thick, glinting blade with a razor-sharp edge firmly affixed to it. When the ride spun the man into view again, the blade sliced through the air only an inch or two below his feet.

Then it rose an inch.

"Help me, goddamn it!" the man cried out as he spun out of view.

Eddie and Jess stood staring. The scene was hard to digest. How had somebody designed this death trap in such a perfect, frightening rhythm? Who had put him here, and were they watching?

All impossible questions to answer.

On the next revolution, the blade sliced clean through a dangling piece of thin chain that hung directly below the soles of the man's shoes.

Only one thing was certain. If Eddie and Jess couldn't free the man in the next minute or two, his feet were next. And judging by the severed chain, a human body would be no match for the deadly contraption.

The man would get sliced like deli meat.

29

Eddie had to act fast or face seeing another gruesome death. A sight worse than Trinity's—if that was even possible. The gut-wrenching notion propelled him forward. Time was quickly running out.

"I'll try and pry him loose!" Eddie shouted to Jess.

He timed his approach to the ride and leapt onto the moving merry-go-round, grabbing a horse's neck to avoid falling.

For a moment, his boots skidded on the slippery wooden planks as he tried to gain traction. Multicolored bulbs flashed in time to the organ's upbeat tones. The mirrored ceiling reflected the dazzling array of lights.

Despite Eddie's disorientation and his lingering grogginess, he found firm footing. He took a moment to compose himself. The platform whizzed around past Jess, who had edged closer to the ride.

"Get me off of here!" the man yelled.

Eddie dragged himself from horse to horse until he reached the man's back. "Jesus Christ," he mumbled as he took in the situation.

The length of chain around the man's ankles had been secured with a sturdy padlock. Heavy-duty handcuffs had been placed around his wrists. Someone had also looped the cuffs through a steel ring that had been welded to the pole, presumably to hold the victim's arms firmly aloft so they couldn't slide down.

These locks are impossible to remove . . .

I don't have much time.

Eddie resorted to brute force. He smashed his forearm against the support pole, but it didn't have even a minuscule effect.

Then he kicked it with all of his might. Nothing.

Eddie slammed his body against the pole, using his full weight.

It didn't budge in the slightest.

There was no chance of breaking the man free in the next few minutes.

The clank of metal on metal split the air. It was the blade cutting off another piece of dangling chain, directly below the man's feet.

"Jess!" Eddie shouted as the ride spun round and round. "The blade!"

She cupped her hand to her ear. "What?"

"Break the blade!"

"Smash the fucking thing!" the terrified man roared.

Jess raced toward the old newsstand. She retrieved a steel pipe from the access tunnel's grate. Sprinted back to the rising apparatus.

Eddie stepped to the edge of the platform, braced himself, and jumped off the ride. He collided with the snow-covered ground, skidding to his knees. His legs battered against a few hidden stones, but he ignored the pain.

The captive man fought against his restraints and gave Jess a wild-eyed stare. "Hit the damned thing!"

She wound up and slammed the metal pole down on the blade, trying desperately to break it or stop its ascent.

A clank rang out. However, the mechanism stayed firmly in place.

Jess battered the piston arm three more times, but it kept rising without ceremony. Smooth, consistent, and deadly.

It was now a fraction of an inch from the man's feet.

"Let me try!" Eddie yelled.

He grabbed the pipe and took a hard swing at the blade.

The impact sent a painful shock wave through his arms. Strong vibrations reverberated through his entire body. He hunched in momentary agony.

"Again!" Jess shouted.

Summoning all his strength, Eddie wound up and swung full force at the blade and piston.

The pipe smashed into the mechanism with an earsplitting clank. And once again, it sent painful shock waves through his body.

But it was no use.

It had caused no damage whatsoever.

The unfazed blade and piston continued to rise.

"Fuck!" Eddie shouted.

"What do we do?" Jess asked.

Eddie thought for a second. "We gotta shut down the ride! There has to be a kill switch somewhere."

"It has to be in the center pole!"

"Right! Go, now! I'll try and lift him up, buy us some more time."

She hesitated for a moment.

"Jess, GO!" Eddie shouted, snapping her out of her haze.

She turned toward the ride and watched as a few of the support poles raced past, getting her timing right. Then she grabbed a pole with both hands and jumped onto the platform.

Jess weaved between the horses and stepped off the moving parts. The center pole was ten feet wide, decorated with elaborate paintwork and oval-shaped mirrors that were surrounded by flashing bulbs.

Eddie watched her fling open a small wooden door, revealing the dark internal space of the ride, and she disappeared inside.

He readied himself and leapt onto the merry-go-round. Navigated his way through the ride to the chained, terrified man.

As he approached, the blade scythed through the air. This time it made contact with the soles of the man's shoes, cutting off a sliver of black rubber.

"Do something!" the man screamed.

Eddie positioned himself behind the pole and wrapped his arms around the man's torso. He tried to lift him up, even if only slightly.

Every second would count.

Every fraction of an inch might buy Jess more time to stop the ride.

"Hurry, Jess!" Eddie shouted, desperately trying to heave the man up.

The blade whipped around again.

The man screamed out in agony. Long, loud, and garbled.

Eddie gazed down at the snow. Blood had sprayed in a circular pattern around the ride.

Something caught his eye on the floor of the merry-go-round. He tried to focus on it. Figure out what he was looking at.

It was the rubber soles of the man's shoes.

One of the pieces had flipped over to show the bottom part. The other sat upright and had a thin slice of the man's foot still inside. It looked like a disgusting piece of uncooked bacon, soaked in blood.

"Jess, hurry!" Eddie cried out, still trying to lift the man ever so slightly.

She didn't respond.

"JESS!" he repeated. "Stop the fucking ride!"

A loud mechanical moan came from the piston arm as it continued its rise.

The ride spun around again.

Desperate, Eddie wrapped his arms around the man's legs and tried to lift.

It was no use.

The blade neared.

A slicing sound whistled through the air.

The man screamed incoherently and flipped like a salmon against the restraints. Blood sprayed from the merry-go-round, staining the snow-covered ground in a gruesome arc.

Even though everything inside told Eddie not to look down, he did.

And he instantly retched.

The man's feet had been sliced off, just above the ankle bone. His severed appendages bumped against the platform. Centrifugal force sent them flying off the ride and plunging into the crimson snow.

Blood pulsed from the man's stumps, staining a second arc in the snow.

"JESS!" Eddie yelled, fighting the urge to vomit at what he was witnessing.

The piston arm moaned again, rising another inch.

The ride spun around again.

The blade neared.

The blade whooshed past.

The man let out an earsplitting scream.

A thicker spray of blood spat out from the merry-go-round. Eddie looked down. The blade had cut off the man's calves. And now, the faster revolutions had a terminal monotony.

The ride spun round again.

The piston arm rose another inch.

Eddie grabbed the cuffs and tried to snap them apart. Smashed the pipe against the padlock. Rammed his heel against the support pole again. Nothing was working.

The ride seemed to be picking up speed, making each cut happen faster and faster. The blade slashed through the man's legs just below his knees. Then directly through his patella. Then through his thigh muscles.

Sections of him dropped and slid across the blood-soaked platform.

The piston arm rose.

The ride spun round.

His legs were nearly gone, carved horizontally in half-inch-thick slices like a New York strip steak.

Eddie turned away and vomited bile. He pulled himself through the ride toward the center pole.

The man screamed from behind him, but Eddie didn't look back.

He rushed inside the center pole's dark space. He felt around the walls for any switches.

Another scream came from outside. Weaker this time.

He and Jess bumped into each other.

"I can't fucking find it!" Jess cried out.

Every few seconds, the flashing lights on the platform lit up the interior of the center pole. A small table had been turned over. A box on the wall was open but had nothing inside. A rug lay bunched to one side.

The man's screaming stopped.

Then, for a heartbeat as the space lit up, Eddie spotted a small hatch on the side wall. He ripped it open, reached inside, and forced down all three levers.

The lights on the ride shut off.

The organ music slowly died out.

Outside, the horses started to slow down until finally the ride came to a stop.

Eddie stood in front of Jess, shaking, covered in his own vomit and the man's blood. This had sunk everything to an unimaginable, obscene level.

Jess sprinted back outside, with Eddie behind her. They weaved through the horses, vaulted off the platform, and moved around to the support pole where the man had been secured.

With the merry-go-round stopped, the town's speakers became the dominant noise, still booming out repeated, warped renditions of "Santa Claus Is Coming to Town."

Radiating light from the Christmas tree bulbs allowed Eddie and Jess to see the full extent of the damage.

Jess covered her mouth in shock.

The man had been sliced horizontally up to his rib cage like a Slinky. His arms hung from the cuffs, but everything below his chest was gone. His head sagged. A thick string of blood dangled from his bottom lip.

The scent of death had overtaken the gingerbread smell of the town. Steaming entrails and sliced body parts had slithered off the merry-go-round and sat in a pile on the snow surrounding the ride.

Eddie's right leg collapsed. He twisted to the side and dry-heaved.

Jess lay crumpled on the frozen ground, her head buried in her hands.

"I'm too late . . ." she mumbled to herself, shaking uncontrollably. "I'm too late . . . I'm too late . . ."

30

Eddie felt numb to everything around him. If a human could be pushed too far, he had reached that point. The cold, the deaths, the fear of never escaping and dying in another terrible trap. The man's pants were blood-coated, and began to crystallize and stiffen from the extreme temperature, repulsing Eddie to his core.

This was all too much to bear.

He knelt down next to Jess. Wrapped a consoling arm around her. It seemed to help, as her shivering slowed and her breathing normalized. But as for him? He was near the point of being beyond redemption.

"I'm sorry," Eddie said.

She looked up at him, tears in her eyes. "I'm sorry too."

He helped her to her feet, and they began to slowly put themselves back together.

After a moment, Jess gazed directly into Eddie's eyes.

"I know who he is," she said, nodding in the direction of the mutilated victim. "It's Damien Hurst. That scumbag serial rapist."

"Are you sure?"

"Yes. You saw his file. And look at his clothes—black cargo pants and a sweater. He's the guy who fought Tank in the church. That's bad news for us."

"Why?"

Jess edged closer to him. "It means that corpse in the forest, the one we thought was *him,* is someone else."

"But . . . there were no other names of victims in the files . . ."

"Exactly. So that means we don't know how many of us have been brought here after all. It also means the killer is still out there."

Eddie considered what she was saying for a moment. "I've been thinking a lot about that. This entire time, we haven't seen anyone else, right? Every death we've witnessed has been a setup, a preplanned trap of some kind. No human contact. No signs of a killer anywhere. You follow?"

"Yes."

"So what, that's the old couple's game? They rig the place and watch from the comfort of their armchairs while we all get slaughtered remotely?"

"Maybe."

He shook his head. "I don't buy it. None of this adds up to me. Something else is going on here, I'm telling you. We just have to figure it out."

"So what do we do?"

"Well, there are two things I know. First, that old couple *cannot* be trusted. There's no way they are just letting us walk right out of here in about . . ."

He looked toward the sky, and reckoned sunrise was approaching. "In about an hour or so. Second thing I know is this: We've spent the past two days on our back foot, reacting. Falling right into their traps around every corner. Getting picked off one at a time."

Eddie studied the deserted town square and festively decorated Main Street. The empty buildings with their brightly lit storefronts. The giant Christmas tree branches swaying in the breeze. The flickering, beautifully adorned lampposts. Snow dancing through the air. He turned back to face Jessica.

"I say it's about time we take our fate into our own hands."

"So what do you propose?" she asked.

"We bust through that perimeter fence before the old couple returns."

"How? It's electrified."

"Remember those railroad ties in the hardware store?"

"Yep."

"We use one to ram the fucking gates. No way they planned for that move."

Jess appeared to ponder his plan for a moment, eventually nodding. "That could work. Plus, you already set off the trap in the hardware store."

"And you saved my ass, if I recall."

"Don't make me do it again." She smiled slightly. "Let's try it."

Eddie and Jess turned in unison and headed through the town square in the direction of the hardware store. In the far distance, a thin slither of lighter blue had appeared on the horizon, signaling the start of the coming day.

They hustled along the sidewalk underneath the row of awnings.

When they reached the store, the door was still ajar from earlier.

"I'll check first this time," she said, with a wink.

Jess went inside and gazed up at the swinging axe mechanism. It hadn't been reset, but this came as no surprise. Like the acid in the wine bottle and Trinity's death in the tunnel, these traps all seemed to be one-shot deals, since nobody in their right mind would make the same mistake twice.

She waved Eddie inside. "All clear."

The floorboards creaked beneath their boots as they entered.

Flashing lights from a streetlamp decoration illuminated the store every second in ambient shades of red and green.

Eddie strode past Jess and headed straight for the back of the store. He weaved around the jumble of boxes and hardware.

She followed, careful not to bump into anything in the murky confines of the store.

He grabbed the top railroad tie from the neat pile in the back and heaved it up. "Jeez, this must weigh a hundred and fifty pounds. That fence stands no chance against this bad boy."

"Want a hand?"

"Sure."

Jess grabbed one end of the heavy wood beam and backed toward the doorway, grunting under the heavy weight.

Within two feet of the store's exit, Eddie suddenly stopped rigid, forcing Jess to stop as well. His eyes widened as he seemed to look at her for some form of confirmation.

"What's the matter?" she asked.

"Did you hear that?"

"Hear what?"

"A click. I swear, something clicked beneath my boot."

She tried to see below the tie. "Whaddya mean?"

"I heard a click, and my right foot dropped an inch." He slowly looked down, fear immediately spreading across his face. "Fucking hell."

"What is it?"

"It looks like . . . a pressure plate."

Jess tentatively dropped to a crouch, keeping a firm grip on her end of the railroad tie. She gazed down. A split second later, the decoration flashed outside, sending the red and green light through the window.

Her eyes widened as wide as Eddie's just had.

"Eddie," she whispered. "Don't move."

31

A cold bead of sweat trickled down Eddie's back. He tried to stay as still as possible, but his arms shook from the heaviness of the railroad tie. This couldn't go on for long without him dropping it. His fatigue had also weakened his ability to think straight. Something had to give.

He looked down at the pressure plate beneath his right foot. He couldn't recall if he'd stepped on the plate on his way into the store.

Did the railroad tie's extra weight trigger it?

Did whoever is out there anticipate this move? How?

Does it matter?

Jess grimaced. "Don't move a muscle, Eddie."

"Likewise please. We shift our weight in any way, we both might get blown to kingdom come."

"You think it's connected to an explosive?"

"It's possible." Eddie rapidly surveyed the ground, trying to track any clues of what the pressure plate was rigged up to.

A thick black cable led from the left side of the plate, extended across the wood floor, and connected to a device on a large, rusty propane tank. It had been secured to the floorboards with thick steel rings.

Another cable ran from the top of the tank to the ceiling and then a few yards overhead. It stopped directly above him.

A formidable steel nozzle pointed directly down at him. A pilot-light flame licked from its muzzle.

"Oh fuck," he muttered.

"The second you step off that plate . . ."

"I'm toast."

Eddie imagined their impending future: They drop the railroad tie and try to run. Suddenly, a powerful jet of fire bursts out of the nozzle, incinerating them in seconds before they can even move a foot.

The memory of his father instantly came to mind—burned to a crisp in an armchair in his own living room, unrecognizable to all, including the people closest to him. The only way they'd made certain it was his dad had been by matching his teeth with dental records from his past. An entire life, reduced to nothing more than a few nondescript molars and fillings from childhood.

And now, history was about to repeat itself. Father and son, both burned by their sins.

Eddie's heart pounded against his chest as he desperately tried to come up with an idea. Anything to avoid getting transformed into a charred skeleton. Despite his deliberations, he could see no way out of the situation.

"I can't hold it for much longer," Jess said, her face straining. Both their arms were quickly weakening under the enormous weight of the railroad tie.

Eddie reached out a leg and stomped on the cable.

It was tough, and firmly secured.

He went to give it a kick.

"Wait!" Jess said.

"What?"

"Breaking that might set off the flamethrower. We have to assume that."

"Yeah," he rasped. "Then what do we do? If either of us

puts this down, the weight distribution changes on my end, and then . . ."

"I know, I know." Jess focused on a wheeled table saw to her left, approximately the same height as her waist. "If I can just . . ."

She reached out with her foot, latched it to the table, and slowly pulled the table saw toward her.

Her arms began to shake from trying to hold the railroad tie steady. It was clear to Eddie that she was moments away from dropping the damned thing and getting them both incinerated.

She grunted, "If I can just balance my end on this . . ."

"Are you sure?"

"No choice. I'm losing it."

Eddie drew in a trembling breath. "Do it, Jess. Quickly"

She delicately rested her end of the tie on the table saw. Then she slowly removed her hands and took a step back, arms trembling.

Nothing happened.

The weight stayed balanced enough, for the moment.

Eddie breathed a sigh of relief. Jess was free of the trap.

But as for me . . .

There was nowhere for him to go. It was *his* foot on the pressure plate. He didn't dare move.

The pilot light still burned directly over his head, waiting for the inevitable moment when Eddie's muscles failed under the strain.

"Great work, Jess," Eddie said, resigned to the situation. "But look. You need to get out of here now."

Jess looked at Eddie for a long moment, considering what he was proposing. Then her face turned to defiance and resolution.

"I'm not ready to give up yet, boss. There's got to be a way to free you too. What if we replace the weight with something else? How much do you weigh?"

"It's not gonna work, Jess. We have no clue how much pressure this railroad tie is adding to my weight, and it's been a long time since I took high school physics. We'd just be guessing."

"Okay. What if I try and disable the propane tank? Stop the flow of gas?"

"You saw what happened to Trinity and Damien. Don't you think they made this shit tamper-proof?" Eddie wheezed, shaking his head. "All you'll do is get both of us killed. I appreciate what you're trying to do, I really do, but the only choice here is for you to save yourself. Now."

"No. I refuse to let you just give up."

"Please, Jess," Eddie implored. "Get out of here before I lose my grip. There's no reason you—"

"Not so fast. I have an idea. I'll run at you full force. You drop the tie and jump away from the plate as I tackle you hard. We might get far enough away from the flame to make it out alive."

"Are you out of your goddamn mind? There's no way."

But he knew it was no use arguing. Jess's face had transformed to one of steely determination. And it gave him a shot at life, instead of a torturous, painful death.

"Ah, fuck," Eddie said. "If this works, I'm going to *seriously* owe you."

"You're damn right you will. But don't thank me yet."

Outside, the darkness of night had started to lift from Old Forge.

The start of Christmas Day.

He let out a bitter laugh at the irony.

"What?" Jess asked.

"Merry Christmas," he said. "Have you had a worse start to the day on Christmas morning?"

"I haven't had many good ones in my life," she replied.

Eddie winced at the pain in his forearms. He wasn't sure how much longer he could hold the railroad tie. It seemed to be growing heavier by the minute.

It felt cruel that he was in touching distance of potential escape from his death. The only way toward it was one suicidal dive. The plan was madness, but there was no talking Jess out of it, clearly.

Eddie looked over his shoulder. "All right, fuck it. Let's do this. On the count of three?"

"You got it."

She hunched down, preparing to run full force.

"One . . ."

Jess dug her heels into the floor.

"Two . . ."

Eddie looked up and said a silent prayer.

"THREE!"

Jess lunged forward and broke into a sprint.

Eddie prepared to drop the railroad tie.

He had to time this perfectly.

She reached within three steps.

He crouched down a few inches, ready to spring forward. And he dropped the railroad tie.

Jess slammed into Eddie hard, wrapping both arms around him, and they flew toward the doorway with tremendous force.

Instantly, the propane ignited, sending a torrent of flames shooting downward to the very spot he had stood a moment ago.

The entire hardware store burst into flames as he and Jess flew through the air.

Intense heat blasted his legs.

For a terrifying moment, flames nearly enveloped his entire body.

The unmistakable smell of burning hair flooded his nostrils.

The red-hot heat from his singed clothes burned against his body.

Eddie and Jess crashed against the floorboards and skidded a few feet past the store's open doorway.

They scrambled to their feet and rushed off the sidewalk, away from the flames.

He didn't look back. Didn't check to see if any part of him was on fire.

Eddie collapsed onto his back.

Wisps of smoke came from his boots and the bottom of his jeans.

Inside the store, a wall of flame came blasting out in all directions, setting fire to everything in sight, the walls and floorboards and all the boxes.

The hardware store was a tinderbox.

Eddie lay on the snowy ground, side by side next to Jess, both trying to catch their breath, utterly exhausted and completely overwhelmed by the moment.

But they were alive.

She saved me again . . .

He looked across to Jess, more grateful than he'd ever before been in his entire life.

"Jess . . . I—"

He never got to finish.

She leaned in and kissed Eddie on the lips.

32

Eddie gently put both his hands on the back of Jess's neck, running his fingers through her hair. He pulled her in closer to his chest.

He closed his eyes and kissed her back.

For a fleeting moment, their world seemed a million miles away from the terror of this place. It felt like they were outside of space and time, and for a moment, the horrors of the past two days faded out of view.

He had developed a strong mental bond with her over the past forty-eight hours. Being this close to death, knowing any second could be their last, still being here with her, had made him feel more alive than he'd ever felt before.

They held each other close, in what seemed like the most intimate, honest moment of his life.

Jess nuzzled into his neck, taking him in, and whispered softly, "Do you think it's possible for us to change who we are?"

Eddie looked deep into her brown eyes. "I have to believe it, Jess. Don't you?"

She paused, staring at the burning building. "I'd like to . . . I'd like to."

She sat up, and Eddie followed suit. Thick black smoke belched into the dawn sky. They backed away from the burning building's strong heat, Eddie trying to process the intimacy of the last few minutes.

"I hope the entire town burns down," Eddie said, smiling.

She grinned back. "I hope *everything* burns down."

As they continued to observe their surroundings, the streetlights blinked off. The lights in the stores vanished. The Christmas music abruptly stopped. All power had left Old Forge, and save for the crackling of the flames, the town became silent.

"I'm guessing that's our signal," Eddie said. "Only one thing left for us to do now."

"Head back to the gate?"

"Head back to the gate," he repeated, resigned to whatever fate had in store for them. No more plans, no more angles. Just a straightforward march toward their meeting with destiny.

They turned and walked together along the cobblestone road. As they drew farther away from the roar of the fire, the sound of songbirds emerged from the trees. The forest was coming alive, as if Nature herself knew it was Christmas morning and was joyously celebrating.

Eddie ignored the frozen corpse and moved deeper into the forest. Jess kept by his side, scanning in all directions.

Ten minutes into the journey, the first shafts of watery winter sunlight speared through gaps in the canopy. The scent of burning was soon replaced by the scent of the woodland.

They rounded a group of trees and came into view of Greg's snow-covered body. Jess led the way, taking a wide path around him, and rounded the side of the concrete bunker.

Eddie checked out the entrance to the underground hub on his way past. It seemed undisturbed since they had left to try to save Damien.

Jess picked up speed along the winding track and under the shadow of the cinder block wall. Maybe it was her building anticipation about what was to come. Eddie shivered, but the cold didn't seem to matter anymore.

Somewhere in the distance, church bells rang seven times. *Civilization.*

As they followed the wall's curving path, the electrified gate came into sight. Jess grabbed Eddie's hand and held it as they cautiously approached.

There, on the other side of the gate, the old couple stood, waiting for their guests to finally arrive.

33

Eddie and Jess stood opposite the old couple. Only the electrified gate separated them, and it still gave off a quiet electric hum. George and Dorothy eyed them through the fence, but gave off no ill will.

"Merry Christmas," George said, seemingly oblivious to what Eddie and Jess had endured for the past two days.

"You said the gates would be open Christmas morning," Eddie replied matter-of-factly. "Were you telling the truth?"

"Yes, we are people of our word." George checked his watch. "The time has come to make good on our promise. But I wonder, did you figure out why you were all brought here, Eddie?"

"Yes."

Dorothy gave him an inquisitive look. "Tell us."

Eddie knew he had to choose his words carefully, not wanting the old couple to have a change of heart in the final moments of his captivity. He said, "Because we've all lived our lives *taking* from others. Lord knows I took . . ."

Eddie's mind drifted off to the old doctor, bleeding out on the floor in front of him so many years ago. He snapped back to the moment at hand.

"I've had more chances to change my behavior than I can count. Sadly, I never did. So as you said yesterday, we are all exactly where we need to be."

George turned to his wife and nodded.

Dorothy met Eddie's gaze. "And when we let you out?"

Eddie looked past the old couple, far away into the distance, toward the rising sun. A flood of memories flashed through his mind. All the wrong choices he made. Every person he stole from. Every life he made worse simply by being born.

"When you let me out . . ." Eddie looked back at George and Dorothy, sincerity in his eyes. "When you let me out, I confess to what I've done. Take responsibility for my actions. Try and undo the damage I've caused. And only after then, I start to build a new life. A better one."

Eddie squeezed Jessica's hand. "We both will."

"Very well," Dorothy said, turning toward her husband. "I, for one, believe him."

"Yes. So do I," George replied, seemingly happy. "Eddie, you are free to go."

With that, George approached the gate, preparing to deactivate the electric current and open it.

"Wait, hold on a second," Eddie said. "We both go. Jess and I."

George gave him a look of sad resignation. "I'm sorry, Eddie, but Jessica cannot leave."

"What? Why? I don't understand. She didn't even do anything! I'm a thief. Tank was a drug dealer. Greg was a con man. Trinity killed a kid in a hit-and-run. Damien, a rapist. We all deserve what we got. But as for Jess—*addiction* isn't a crime. It's a disease."

George slowly nodded in agreement. "Yes, it is a disease. One that we know cannot be cured."

"Bullshit," Eddie shot back. "You have to let her at least try!"

"What do you think, honey?" George asked Jess with sadness in his eyes. "Do you think you can change?"

Jess slowly looked down and let go of Eddie's hand.

After a moment, she shook her head *no*.

Baffled, Eddie turned to her. "I don't get it, Jess. What's your addiction?"

She stared deep into his eyes. "Eddie, I'm sorry. I . . ."

"What?"

She took a deep breath in, and slowly exhaled.

"I'm a serial killer."

Jess plunged a knife hard into Eddie's guts.

He stared back at her, wide-eyed, paralyzed with pain and shock.

His mind couldn't comprehend what had just happened. However, his body reacted. His legs buckled and his back slammed hard against the ground, knocking the wind out of him.

His vision blurred, but not before he saw Jess hunched over him, gazing down at him with the curiosity of a snake looking into a bird's nest.

Jess leaned down to pull out the knife. The suction from Eddie's body held it in place. She planted her boot against his chest and heaved the blade free, causing massive internal bleeding on the way out.

Eddie tried to speak, but only managed a rasping stutter.

Jess put a finger to his lips and then gently caressed his face.

She stared into his eyes, watching the life slowly drain from them.

The feelings this sight evoked, and the need to keep seeing it again and again, would never leave her. About that part of her addiction, she had told Eddie the truth. But it didn't stop the pangs of guilt and remorse tugging at her every sense.

I owe him the truth.

She leaned down close to him, tears now fully streaming down her face.

"I am so, so sorry, Eddie."

"Why?" he quietly asked her, as blood filled his mouth.

"This place . . . this *hunt*. It's the only way my parents could . . . *contain* . . . my urges. So I stay in here, a prison of my own design, to be free to be my true self. Do you understand?"

Eddie shook his head. His confusion came as no surprise to her.

"My parents have sacrificed so much for me. And you've sacrificed so much, Eddie. But it's better I be in here than out there at the mercy of my own . . . demons."

Jess's tears dripped from her cheek and landed on Eddie's heaving chest. He struggled for breath. The knife had likely pierced one of his lungs.

"For what it's worth," Jess continued, "I too believe you. That you would have changed, if given the chance."

Eddie's glassy-eyed stare cut deep.

"I wish . . ." she said through her tears. "I wish I could say the same about myself."

She clutched his hand and held it delicately, her experience telling her that there were only moments to go before . . .

Eddie's breathing became shallow.

Tears welled in his eyes.

He squeezed her hand in return, perhaps searching for comfort in his final moments. But his trembling stopped.

Seconds later, Eddie's eyes flickered shut.

He was gone, experience told her.

Jess shuddered from the rush that raced through her body. Nothing else in the world came remotely close to matching this sensation. Although this one felt different, more painful than the others.

After a moment of silence kneeling over his body, Jess rose to a standing position. She gazed at Eddie for a few more seconds. He remained lifeless. Blood had pooled by the left side of his coat, and his complexion had turned ghostly white.

The gate's electric hum abruptly stopped.

Jess stepped over his corpse and pushed open the gate, sorrow in her face.

"Mom, Dad, I am sorry you had to see that. I just couldn't bring myself earlier to . . ."

Dorothy looked away from the scene, forlorn. She said, "I don't want to speak of it, honey."

Jess nodded. "I understand."

George took a step toward his daughter and wrapped his arms around her. "Merry Christmas, sweetie."

Jess cherished the warm embrace, holding him tight for several seconds. She moved across to her mom and hugged her.

"Merry Christmas," she whispered.

Dorothy let go of her daughter and took a step back. A tear ran down her cheek as she looked away once again.

This part always hurt Jess deep inside. Their annual embrace on Christmas Day morning. Her only gift. The closest her parents would ever let her get since consigning her to a life in the replicated town of Old Forge.

But as upsetting as it was for all of them, there was no other choice.

It was better to have this yearly fleeting moment in time—after satisfying her undeniable urges—than to share the same moment in a prison visiting room, incarcerated for killing countless innocents.

34

et up.

A voice inside Eddie's head screamed at him to move. But he had no strength. For a second, he had no idea where he was. A jumble of mismatched memories flooded his mind. The first sight of his dead father. The constant disappointment in his mother's eyes. Visiting his brother before Christmas. A grocery store in Old Forge. A conversation between a daughter and her parents.

Jess.

George and Dorothy.

The betrayal at the gates.

His memories crystallized into a single, chilling moment.

Being stabbed.

At that moment, a wave of energy pulsed through his body.

Eddie's eyes snapped open as he lay on the ground, bleeding out. He caressed his wounded stomach. It felt like somebody had run him through with a medieval lance. But he sensed an opportunity to escape. One shot at survival. If he could just make it far enough away before collapsing again.

He looked at the gate.

It was open.

Jess and her parents stood close to one another, like a family that had just gone out for an early morning walk. Anger flared inside him. He balled his fists.

This was his one and only moment.

He had to move fast, hit hard, and run for his life.

Eddie wrestled himself up. He ignored the unbearable pain in his stomach and his immense difficulty breathing. The numbness in his body from lying on the snow. He was now a man with nothing to lose. And he had pure hatred for the obstacles in his path.

The parents spotted his movement immediately.

But he had already started sprinting.

"Jess!" George yelled.

She spun to face him.

Eddie thrust his boot toward her gut.

He gave the strike everything he had and pounded his heel against her midsection, sending her flying back. He stumbled a few paces forward, bringing him within inches of George and Dorothy. Eddie barreled between the old couple, sending them both stumbling backward. He clutched his stomach as he raced in the direction of the farmhouse.

Every step increased his agony.

He headed to the left of the farmhouse, past a deserted chicken coop. Eddie dared to look back. None of the twisted family had given chase. Yet.

Jess helped her parents regain their balance. All three stared in his direction.

He headed past a large barn with open doors.

Inside the brightly lit space, in the far-left corner of the building, six gurneys had been neatly lined up. Each had a table which held monitoring equipment and an intravenous drip. On the right side, an open door led to what looked like a small parking lot.

Eddie swerved inside the barn and out of sight.

Supplies had been stacked to his left. Various cans of food, dried pasta, cookies, huge containers of mineral water. To his right, hundreds of items sat on a long wooden table. Watches, jewelry, and other trinkets. He didn't experience the slightest urge to take anything.

The wooden stove next to the valuables had a large pile of ash inside. He guessed that was where George incinerated victims' wallets and IDs.

Many of the items in the barn were protected by dusty sheets.

Eddie staggered past enough evidence to ensure the family would spend the rest of their lives in prison, but his only priority was leaving the farm and getting medical treatment fast. Their time would come soon enough.

He gasped out breaths as he headed through the doorway, back into the low sunshine of Christmas morning. And he came face-to-face with roughly forty vehicles, mostly snow-covered and partially hidden by camouflaged netting. The closest models looked at least ten years old, but newer models were in the rows near the back.

Eddie had never acquired the skill to hot-wire a car. He wasn't even sure if it was still possible with modern vehicles.

At the very back, he spotted his SUV.

The sight chilled him to his core, but he had to keep moving.

Beyond the small parking lot, tire tracks in the snow led to a distant road.

He remembered the church bells.

Some form of life had to be close.

A strong shooting pain knocked the wind out of Eddie. He hunched for a second next to the front row of cars. Then he grabbed the roof of the closest one and hauled himself forward, using the stationary vehicles for support.

Sweat beaded his brow.

He drew in deep breaths.

Grimaced from the shooting pains in his gut.

It felt like he was going too slow—Jess and her parents were bound to catch up with him soon. But he had no other choice. Eddie doubted he had the physical strength to stand and fight for any length of time.

He cleared the small parking lot and joined the tire tracks. He knew they had been made very recently, because last night's snow would have obscured them.

Only fifty yards to the road.

His run had turned into a fast limp. Warm blood glistened on his hand, but he kept it firmly pressed against his injury. He left a trail of blood in the snowy ground behind him.

Eddie tried to process the last day. The last twenty minutes.

How could I have missed this?

It was Jess the entire time.

Orchestrating everything.

The way she looked into my eyes after stabbing me.

He cast his mind back to Tank's death in the church. Jess had crouched over his body as he took a final, bubbling breath. She had also knelt by Greg when he died as a result of the bear's savage attack. And Trinity . . . Jess and him had both stared down at that horrific moment.

And then there was Damien Hurst. He began to see his death in an entirely different light. How upset Jess had been when she missed his last moment alive.

How could I have been so stupid?

Jess had been assertive but taken a backseat, encouraging them toward each of the traps with reasoned argument. With the benefit of hindsight, her actions seemed obvious, though nobody had had the faintest idea.

Was she legitimately unconscious when I found her in the back of the saloon?

Or did she bash herself over her head to play the part of a fellow victim?

Right now, the answer to these questions didn't matter.

Eddie stumbled a few more wheezing steps and hit a country lane. He took a moment to catch his breath, frantically looking in both directions. One way led to snowy hills. The other to flatter land.

He glanced back at the tire tracks, farmhouse, and barn.

So far, the family had not followed.

It came as a relief, but he knew his survival still hung in the balance.

Eddie took off again, hobbling along the side of the road, hoping for any sign of salvation.

A few lung-busting minutes later, he detected the sound of a vehicle.

For a terrifying second, he thought it had come from the direction of the farmhouse. However, as the roar of an engine became louder, he realized it was coming from the direction he was heading.

Headlights stabbed around the corner of the misty lane.

Eddie lurched into the middle of the road, waving his arms, shouting for the approaching vehicle to stop.

A police cruiser raced toward him at high speed.

The relief almost sent him crashing to his knees.

The cruiser's tires skidded, stopping directly in front of him.

He was saved.

35

Eddie struggled around to the driver's side of the cruiser. The window lowered with an electric whine, letting out a blast of heat. A lone cop sat behind the wheel. He looked middle-aged and stern, and was wearing a thick black coat.

"Whoa, whoa, whoa," the cop shouted. "What are you doin' out here, son?"

For a moment, Eddie was at a loss for words. He wanted to say a thousand different things. Blurt out the full story as concisely as possible.

The cop looked at his bloodstained hand, covering the knife wound. "Are you hurt?"

"Please, Officer," Eddie said rapidly. "You need to help me. Now!"

"Slow down. What happened?"

Eddie tried to compose himself through the pain. He needed his next words to be clearly understood and acted upon. "I was kidnapped and held against my will for the past three days right down the road in this, like, compound."

"Kidnapped? By who?"

"By this crazy old couple and their psycho daughter. They've been doing it for years, killing people—"

"Wait, hold on a second, son." The cop released his seat belt and climbed out of the car. "Now, nice and slowly. Tell me what happened."

Eddie tried to speak more calmly. "Look, Officer, I need immediate medical attention. Please."

The cop nodded. "And we'll deal with that in just a second. First though, who's been killing who?"

"I was kidnapped in Old Forge three days ago. There were others too, but I'm the only one left alive. It happened less than a mile from here, this couple and their daughter."

The cop motioned his head in the direction of the farmhouse. "That way?"

"That's right. They built a replica town in the forest and use it to hunt people every year." Eddie winced. "I know this sounds crazy but . . . Jesus Christ. Take me to a hospital and I'll tell you everything."

The cop gave him a skeptical frown. "Look, son. The only people that live down that way are the Kanes. And they are *not* the kidnapping type. They're a respected family that's lived in these parts for decades. And their daughter left home years ago. So forgive me doubting your bullshit story, but . . . are you on something?"

"No." Eddie growled in frustration. "I know it seems unbelievable. Take me to the hospital and I'll explain the whole thing."

"Okay, okay. Here, let me help you. Get in the back of the car."

Eddie breathed a sigh of relief. "Thank you."

He climbed into the back of the warm cruiser and sat delicately on the backseat. He pressed firmly on the wound in his gut, praying he didn't bleed out before making it to the hospital.

The cop jumped behind the wheel, and the door locks popped down.

"What's your name, son?" the cop asked in the rearview mirror.

"Eddie. Eddie Parker."

"Where are you from, Eddie?"

"Fort Drum?"

"And how did you end up in our little town of Old Forge?"

"I was just passing through and stopped off for a pack of smokes. Wait . . . are we close to town?"

"A couple of miles. Back the way I came. All right, let's get going."

The cruiser's engine purred to life, and the cop shifted the car into drive. He carefully drove forward along the snow-covered road.

Back in the direction of the farmhouse.

"Wait. Is this the way to the hospital?" Eddie asked.

"Oh, we'll get there soon enough. But we're only a minute from George and Dorothy's. I'd like to get to the bottom of this first."

Eddie sat forward. "Are you shitting me? Turn around."

Ignoring him, the cop continued to drive.

"Turn the goddamn car around!"

Again, the cop ignored him.

The road to the farmhouse loomed just ahead. The cop flicked on his turn signal. Eddie slammed his fists into the plastic partition that separated him from the front seat, sending excruciating pain shooting through him.

He grabbed the door handle and yanked.

Nothing.

Slammed on the window. Nothing but pain in his fist.

"Turn the fucking car around!"

The cop silently shook his head. He navigated the cruiser

past the side of the farmhouse. George and Dorothy had made their way back from the electrified gate. They stood by their back door, looking serious.

The sight of the old couple, along with the pain in his chest, made Eddie want to vomit over the backseat. Jess was nowhere to be seen. He sank lower, hoping the tinted windows would hide his presence.

"All right, gimme a minute, Eddie Parker," the cop said. "Let's see what's really going on here."

Without hesitation, the police officer jumped out of the car and headed toward George and Dorothy, his hand resting on his holster.

This, at least, seemed like the correct approach. Eddie carefully peered through the windows, trying to hide himself as much as possible, hopeful that the cop would arrest them. A simple search of the property would reveal all their darkest secrets.

The cop held an animated conversation with the elderly couple for a few minutes, motioning back at the police cruiser several times.

Eddie's heart pounded. At any moment, he expected Jess to spring from behind the farmhouse and stab the cop.

But she never appeared.

Eventually, the officer turned and headed back toward the car, his boots crunching against the frozen ground. The old couple remained on their doorstep, peering toward the cruiser. This evidently wasn't over.

What's going on?

The police officer approached the vehicle. He flung open the back door.

"Why haven't you arrested them yet?" Eddie demanded. "Look in the barn if you need evidence!"

The officer stared down at Eddie with a stern look. "You know, Mr. Parker, Old Forge has the lowest crime rate in New York State. And no homicides for thirteen years in a row. A fact I'm very proud of. And you know how we keep that crime rate so low?"

The cop's words jogged Eddie's memory. He had heard this before. A look of realization spread across his face.

"Wait . . . you're . . . the sheriff?"

"Indeed, son. Saw you a few days ago in the grocery store, when you were trying to steal from these good folks."

"Look—"

"Get out of the car, son."

"What?"

The cop whipped a revolver out of its holster. He leveled the gun at Eddie's face. "Get out of the car. Slowly."

Eddie shook his head. "Whaddaya mean? You can't be serious?"

The cop leaned in and grabbed the shoulder of his coat.

"What the hell?" Eddie yelled.

"Get the fuck out," the sheriff replied through clenched teeth. Then he dragged Eddie out of the car, shoved him, and aimed the gun at his face again. "Now walk."

Eddie backed away a couple of steps, palms raised defensively. "I don't know what the hell they told you, but I'm the victim here."

"You're the victim?" The sheriff laughed. "You've been a scourge on the community your whole life, son. This was only ever going to end one way. Your card has been marked for a long time. Now walk, or I shoot you here on the spot."

He looked between the cop and George and Dorothy. The

old couple silently watched. Neither looked happy or sad. Just resigned to whatever was in store.

Eddie sank to his knees.

All hope had been crushed in a matter of minutes.

He had no idea what to do. He feared for his life more than at any time during the last twenty-four hours.

"Back on your feet," Sheriff Briggs ordered. "Right now."

Eddie looked up at him. "Please. You're a police officer. These people are responsible for the deaths of—"

"Of many, many criminals. I can sleep easy knowing that."

"You're insane."

Sheriff Briggs pulled back his revolver's hammer. "Five. Four. Three. Two."

Eddie gingerly climbed to his feet. He turned toward the imposing wall that surrounded Jess's version of Old Forge.

Briggs pushed him forward.

He stumbled a few steps, struggling for breath.

George and Dorothy joined the sheriff and followed him across the field toward the compound. None of them uttered a word.

Eddie headed through the gates without looking back. They immediately clanked the fence shut behind him, and seconds later, an electric hum filled the air.

He was trapped inside the compound once again. Dorothy, George, and Sheriff Briggs turned and walked back toward the farmhouse. None of them seemed remotely interested in his fate.

To Eddie's left, Jess stood leaning against a huge pine tree, bloodied knife still in her hand. He glared at her in silence.

Her knife glinted in the rising sun.

"I'm sorry, Eddie, I truly am," Jess finally said. "I'm going to give you an hour's head start. You've earned at least that much."

Eddie hung his head low, resigned to what was coming in the next few hours.

This was never how he'd imagined things would end.

Jess would never change. And his change had come too late.

"Best get going now," she implored.

Soaked in his blood, and coughing through his labored breathing, Eddie limped his way into the forest, looking back every few seconds to ensure Jess had not yet followed.

And as he trekked deeper into the forest, deeper into this prison built by his lifetime of mistakes, all he could hear was that one lone Christmas song, lazily wafting on the breeze, coming from the town's distant speakers . . .

Ohhh . . . You better watch out . . .

EPILOGUE

January 28th

Maria Fontana leaned back in her office chair. Outside the window, light snow fell on Van Am quad. Columbia University students hurried along the paths, rushing back to their dorms after their final classes.

Her students were her number one priority, once again. Returning to work as the head of Columbia's Psychology Department had been a welcome return to normality. Especially since the events of a few years earlier, when she had helped catch the serial killer Wyatt Butler on a transatlantic cruise, and barely escaped with her life. And the lives of her children.

But since then, the FBI had come calling at regular intervals for a second opinion on their psychological profiles for impossible-to-crack criminal investigations.

To date, though, this was the only time *she* called them first. It was about something the FBI—and very likely everyone else—had missed.

Footsteps pounded along the corridor, heading toward her office. The last meeting of the day promised to be her most important one.

Someone knocked on the door three times. Short and regimented. The calling card of Agent Chris Spear from the FBI.

"Come in," she called out.

Spear entered the room, with his usual neat goatee, sharp suit, and circular glasses that evoked a bygone age. He smiled at her. "Good to see you, Maria."

"Likewise. Have a seat, Chris."

"How are the kids?"

"Doing great. In their junior year of high school, if you can believe it."

"Good, good," Spear replied, smiling. "So . . . you said you needed to talk. How can I help you?"

Maria pushed a file folder across her desk toward the agent.

He opened the folder, containing clippings from various Upstate New York newspapers spanning a dozen years or so.

"I think it's me that can help *you*," Maria said. "Upstate New York, a small hamlet named Old Forge. The town has less than a thousand people living in it."

"Okay," Spear murmured, still scanning all the newspaper clippings.

"Barely any crime to speak of, which is fairly normal for a town as tightly knit as this. But that's not what caught my attention a few months ago."

"Go on."

"Every year, right around Christmastime, half a dozen people go missing in the areas surrounding Old Forge. I tracked it back fourteen years. Every year, like clockwork. This past Christmas was no different."

"Well, that in itself isn't that unusual, Maria. You know suicides spike around the holidays. Half these people probably go on a hike with no intention of ever coming back."

"Maybe. Maybe not. But when I looked more closely at the disappearances, I noticed something very odd. All these folks, nearly a hundred over the past fourteen years, have a criminal past of some kind. All unrelated to each other. The only thing that connects their disappearances is geography. The approximate area they were seen last."

"Old Forge."

"Old Forge, New York." Maria gave him an affirmative nod. "And every single one . . . a criminal."

Spear rubbed his chin, considering.

"C'mon, Chris. I don't believe in coincidences."

"So, what you're saying is . . ."

Maria looked at the FBI agent with an intensity in her eyes. "This is the work of a serial killer. Quite possibly the most *prolific* serial killer in American history, one who has masterfully evaded detection for more than a decade. And, worse for us, one who clearly has *no* intention of stopping."

"I see," Spear said, closing the file folder and sliding it back across the desk. "So then it's up to you and me to stop him."

"You're damn right it is."

Agent Spear nodded his head in agreement.

"Then, let's get started."

ACKNOWLEDGMENTS

JAMES MURRAY

The best part of writing novels has been becoming best friends with my cowriter, Darren, over the past eight years. I literally cannot imagine my life without him in it. He is thoughtful, kind, hilarious, and one hell of a writer.

Thanks to our excellent editor, Michael Homler, and the entire St. Martin's team for their continued partnership. Thanks to my colleagues and friends Joseph, Nicole, and Ethan for their imagination and support. Thanks to Jack Rovner and Dexter Scott from Vector Management; Brandi Bowles and our entire team from UTA; Danny Passman from GTRB; and Mitch Pearlstein and Cristian Hitchcock from PSBM. And special thanks to Brad Meltzer, R.L. Stine, Clay McLeod Chapman, and James Rollins for their continued mentorship, advice, and friendship.

And most important, thanks to my incredible wife, Melyssa, the most thoughtful, caring person I know. I love you.

And finally, thanks to all the amazing *Impractical Jokers* fans around the world—we hope you love this thriller as much as we enjoyed writing it!

DARREN WEARMOUTH

First, I'd like to thank my coauthor, James. Besides being a great guy, he's a best friend who I value deeply. Every time I cross the southern border to work on our books, James and Melyssa are always kind and generous hosts who go above and beyond. They are truly my American family; I treasure our time together.

Second, Michael Homler, our editor from St. Martin's Press, and his extended team who make the publishing process a pleasure. Michael is a considerate and excellent editor.

Third, I'd like to acknowledge the close and extended family that James and I have sadly lost during the creation of this book. Loss is never easy, but I've been incredibly proud of James during this period. They will live forever in our hearts.

On a personal level, I always leave my wife and daughter, Jen and Maple, to the end. No real words can sum up how much they mean to me. Seeing a smile on their faces is enough to keep me flying.

Last, and most important, a huge thanks to you for reading *You Better Watch Out*. We know how much time you have invested to read our work and it's deeply appreciated.

ABOUT THE AUTHORS

Courtesy of truTV

Jennifer Wearmouth

James S. Murray is a writer, executive producer, and actor, best known as "Murr" on the hit television show *Impractical Jokers* on truTV and TBS. He is the owner of Impractical Productions, LLC, and co-owner of Bad Woods Entertainment. He is the author of the international bestselling Awakened trilogy, the thrillers *Don't Move* and *The Stowaway*, and the children's sci-fi book series Area 51 Interns. Originally from Staten Island, James now lives in Princeton, New Jersey, with his wife, Melyssa, and dogs, Penny and Pepper.

    Instagram / Threads: @TheRealMurr
    TikTok: @JamesMurrayJokers
    Facebook / X: @JamesSMurray

Darren Wearmouth is the author of numerous international bestselling novels, including the Awakened trilogy, *First Activation, Critical Dawn,* and *The Stowaway*. He is a member of the International Thriller Writers group and lives in Canada with his wife and daughter.

    FB / X / IG @darrenwearmouth